A NATION WITHOUT

The History America Forgot

Mack E. Smith

Sara Freeman Smith

ISBN: 978-0-9662328-9-9

Library of Congress Control Number has been applied for.

Unacknowledged quotations are by Mack E. Smith and Sara Freeman Smith.

Publisher's Cataloging-in-Publication

Names: Smith, Mack E., author. | Smith, Sara Freeman, author.
Title: A Nation Without: The History America Forgot / Mack E. Smith, Sara Freeman Smith.
Description: Houston, TX: U R Gems LLC, 2026.
Identifiers: LCCN: 2026901414 | ISBN: 9780966232899 (paperback) | 9798994660904 (hardcover) | 9780966232820 (eBook)
Subjects: LCSH: United States--History. | Minorities--History--United States. | African Americans--History. | Indigenous peoples--History--United States. | Cultural awareness--United States. | Visions. | LCGFT: Fiction. | BISAC: FICTION / African American & Black / Historical. | FICTION / Cultural Heritage. | FICTION / Indigenous / Historical.
Classification: LCC: PS3619.M59173 N38 2026 | DDC: 813/.6--dc23

(Provided by Cassidy Cataloguing Services, Inc.)

For information about special discounts for bulk purchases, please contact U R Gems LLC at info@ urgems.com.

Dedication

To Rashod, Amy, Alexander, Miles, and Keaton – always remember the marginalized and pass the message on!

To the memory and eternal spirit of Willie Mae Pendleton. She imparted her drive, determination, and persistence in overcoming unthinkable obstacles. Through her, we learned the power of education, the fruits inherited in hard work, and real compassion for others.

To every unsung minority and immigrant overlooked in history for their ingenuity and vital contributions to America.

Acknowledgments

Thank you God for the courage to write what we believe.

Love you Mack for not giving up on the vision God gave you!

Thank you Ella D. Curry and your fantastic team at EDC Creations Media Group for making this dream a reality! Each of you are Gems!

Thanks to Sherian Brown, our awesome editor, for all her diligent work.

A special thanks goes to Tia Ross and the Black Writers Collective for the work they do to support writers.

Table of Contents

Chapter 1

The Hollow Success

Bobby Phillips's office was as cool and smooth as the guy himself. Floor-to-ceiling windows overlooked a midsize American city's skyline, one he rarely took time to see even though his firm owned half the billboards looming over the streets. Traffic inched its way through downtown like a sluggish river below, but Bobby never even looked down. He preferred to look at himself.

A temple of his power, his office was built of glass, chrome, and leather fashioned into an atmosphere so precise it made visitors unconsciously stiffen their backs. Everything echoed the light of hidden lamps, polished every day by a staff he never acknowledged. The atmosphere contained the faintest whiff of leather and steel, a calculated sterility intended to impart control. To Bobby, the office was not an office but proof of his brilliance and a testament to his mastery.

"Presentation?" he growled. His voice cracked across the room like a lash.

He dropped a chunky binder onto the conference table, papers scattering in every direction, before the binder slid along the tabletop to thud onto the floor in a burst of crumpling paper. His intern, a wide-eyed young woman fresh out of graduate school, flinched at the crash, her knuckles whitening as she struggled to compose herself.

"This is to impress potential investors?" Bobby inquired. "Amateur hour. If I wanted mediocre work, I'd hire from the civil service."

He chuckled at his words. Nobody else did.

At the far side of the table, his cousin Richard shifted uneasily. They had once been as close as a couple of kids playing ball in the park and trading secrets at family gatherings. Now Richard was hardly more than a paperweight with the Phillips name engraved on his business card. His role with the firm was a title, the family name kept prominent on the masthead by its bestowal.

"Bobby, the numbers are fine," Richard said cautiously. "The staff has worked overtime for the last week. Maybe what it needs is some shine, not—"

"Not excuses," Bobby cut in roughly. He pointed a finger like a dagger. "Do not forget you are here because of me. My father started this company, his father before him, and now me. It is in our blood to command. You," he jabbed again, "would be peddling insurance if it weren't for our name."

The room fell silent. The employees exchanged hurried glances. One of the young analysts pressed her lips together, holding back an insult. Another lowered his eyes and tapped his pen on the table to hide his anger. Resentment glowed in the silence, but none of them had the courage to speak. They knew Bobby hated slights like men did birthdays.

Richard leaned forward again, his tone low. "You are burning bridges, Bobby. Even with family."

"Family." Bobby snorted, readjusting his tie. "Family is dead weight unless they pull their own. That's what my father told me. I live by it."

Richard scowled. "Maybe that's why your wife left you and why your kids don't call."

Bobby's eyes narrowed into a sinister glare. "Watch yourself, Richard. You are here as a courtesy, not a necessity. Don't confuse family history with relevance today."

Richard leaned back, lips clenched into a line. He had seen this version of Bobby too many times, the version that devoured loyalty and cast it aside.

Bobby rose as he fastened the buttons of his suit jacket. In the dark-tinted window, he was struck by his image—a thin man with graying hair and a jaw drawn in habitual contempt. The very embodiment of American know-how, at least according to the magazines. He thought so himself. Each piece of press lauding his daring leadership was an anthem to his genius. Forget the long nights, the reduced salaries, the deceptions endured by those who followed him. Their labor was unseen, as it ought to be. The empire bore his name, not theirs.

He adjusted his cufflinks and pushed aside the papers scattered on the carpet. "Clear up this mess," he told his intern. "I have a gala to attend. Maybe there I will meet people who know quality."

Her cheeks flushed with embarrassment as she bent to retrieve the binder. Bobby didn't even glance in her direction as he headed toward the door.

The conference room was still as the heavy door swung shut behind him. For a moment, nobody shifted. Then Richard breathed out slowly, rubbing at his thinning hair.

"He hasn't changed," Richard growled.

Down the hallway, Bobby's shoes clicked against marble. His mind was already racing ahead to the gala, where he would deliver his address on American ingenuity and remind his peers why his name deserved to dominate the morning papers. Behind him, the resentment of his staff hung over him like a cloud, but Bobby didn't notice it. He never did.

The ballroom was ablaze with crystal chandeliers and immaculately polished marble floors. Black-jacketed waiters darted between tables, their trays of champagne glasses glinting like liquid fire. Banners dangled from the ceiling, the bold letters of the night's theme written in glittering script: *Celebrating American Ingenuity.*

Guests filled the room, their gowns billowing across the polished floor, their tuxedos white and sharp. The atmosphere pulsed with the hum of conversation, the clinking of silver, and the faraway playing of a string quartet in the corner. Everyone was there to be noticed, but few did it as self-assuredly as Bobby Phillips.

Bobby strode in as if the gala was being presented in his name, and to Bobby, it was. His tuxedo was pleated to the mark, his shoes gleaming until they rivaled the chandeliers above. He strode into the entrance without apology, shoving a waiter aside who nearly dropped a tray before scurrying out of the way. He did not look around to catch sight of the man saving himself. Bobby did not pay attention to the individuals who created opportunities.

"Mr. Phillips." The emcee beckoned forward, beaming with a high-gloss smile honed over two decades. She clutched a clipboard to her bosom and spoke in measured, cheerful tones. "We're delighted to have you with us tonight."

"Sure you are," Bobby replied smoothly. "It's not every day you get a keynote speaker who built a kingdom from scratch."

Her smile wavered, the corners cracking for a moment, before stabilizing again. Drawing him with her, she glided toward the head table. Bobby brought up the rear, drinking in the heads turning, the whispers, and the awkward silence that clung to him like a wave.

Across the table, heads nodded in recognition: CEOs, politicians, high-dollar donors. Bobby sat down, his spine straight, his eyes roving the room like a general surveying troops. The brief silence given to him was satisfying. It reminded him of how much influence he held by simply being there.

Dinner was served in impeccable courses. Roasted duck breast, airy soufflés, and desserts were set out like works of art. Bobby shoveled food around his plate without eating. His mind was on the speech he was to deliver mere moments from now. He pictured the applause echoing through the ballroom, the favorable coverage in tomorrow's business page, and the mixture of jealousy and respect set upon the faces of his rivals.

As the time came, he was ushered in by the emcee, and Bobby rose from his seat with a practiced smile. He walked up to the podium with the poise of someone destined to be watched. The crowd was half-hearted in their applause as he adjusted the microphone.

"Ladies and gentlemen," he began, his tone smooth and echoing over the speakers, "we are here tonight to honor what has rendered this nation the best in the books. Ingenuity. Innovation. The sheer determination of leadership that won't give up."

Whispers ceased. Heads turned. Bobby had the cadence of a seasoned speaker, confident and commanding.

"I stand before you today as proof of what determination can achieve. I built Phillips Media from the ground up into a global contender on my terms and with my work ethic. My family kept this torch burning across generations. We succeed because success is in our blood. It's what we do."

A polite round of applause ensued. Bobby smiled, soaking it up.

"And let us not forget," he continued, "that America prospers because of individuals who are risk-takers, go against the conventional, and do not spend too much time on excuses. Too many individuals want to be given credit for merely showing up. But progress is not made on excuses. Progress is made by leaders who will do what others won't."

A professor leaned over a side table. A Latina businesswoman glared at her husband. None of it was noticed by Bobby.

"There are those who claim our prosperity rests on the shoulders of so-called marginalized groups: immigrants, workers, activists. I respectfully say America wasn't built on grievances or entitlements. It was built on visionaries, on families like mine that know hard work and leadership."

The air grew taut. Glasses clinked gently as the waiters refilled them, attempting to bridge the sudden tension.

Across a table, an African American professional young woman stretched out to her co-worker, murmuring something grooved with a scowl.

Bobby noticed the gesture and took it. "Yes," he sneered, "we all play our part. Some provide ideas, others provide sweat. But let us be honest. Without leaders to pilot the ship, the labor means nothing. That is the definition of ingenuity."

Applause broke out again, though ragged and uneven. Bobby didn't notice, or perhaps he didn't care. His chest expanded with pride as he rode his speech home.

"So tonight," he declared, his hand reaching up slightly, "let us honor the brave who lead, the bold who innovate, and those who are called upon to carry America's legacy of greatness forward. Thank you."

The subsequent applause was tense, even courteous. Satisfied, Bobby returned to his seat.

At the table, one of the executives leaned over to him. "Harsh words, Bobby."

"Truth hurts occasionally," answered Bobby, swirling his wine. "People need to be reminded who does the heavy lifting in this country."

Across from him, another businessman tilted his head. "And you don't count immigrants or minorities in that category?"

Bobby laughed loudly enough for the tables around them to overhear. "They have their role, sure. But greatness is born of vision, not sweat. History credits the visionaries, not the grunts bolting things together."

The words lingered, tainting the air. The people around them immediately diverted their conversation to other topics. The professor at the nearby side table got up early. The Latina businesswoman gazed into her glass. The African American professional departed before dessert.

Bobby sat back, smiling to himself. With courage, he had said what he believed to be the truth. Indeed, he had exposed himself, his arrogance, his blindness, and his insensitivity to the very people whose shoulders he had stood upon.

As the evening drew to a close and visitors headed for the door, Bobby rose, brushing crumbs from his jacket. He adjusted his cufflinks, appreciated the reflected glint of the chandelier in his glass of wine, and walked out of the ballroom as though the evening had crowned him king.

The evening ended with standard handshakes and choreographed photographs. His rehearsed smile never faltering, Bobby posed with executives and donors. He signed a silent auction check but made sure the cameras got the shot, holding his pen so the logo reflected in the flash. Charity wasn't generosity in Bobby's world. It was just another tool, another way of polishing his image for tomorrow's press.

As the guests trickled out, rumors buzzed with strained courtesy. Ears caught polite words strained with unease. People described his speech in guarded voices, the kind people use when they do not wish to offend a man in authority. Bobby missed the unease entirely and saw the evening as a victory.

A server leaned over to another by the kitchen doors and shook his head. A professor left, rolling his eyes in disgust. The Latina executive who had stiffened during Bobby's presentation did not wait to bid farewell. None of it reached Bobby's eyes.

Outside, in the light of streetlamps, valets hurried and turned keys, moving cars around in a compact line of headlights. Marcus waited in a black sedan, engine purring, door open. He'd driven Bobby for years, putting up with tantrums and condescension with steady forbearance most would have given up. Bobby did not notice the cold stare the driver directed at him. This evening, Bobby was in spectacularly good humor, riding high on what he saw as a victory.

"Finally," Bobby growled, getting into the back seat. "I told you I wanted the car ready when I came out. Can't you tell time?"

"Sorry, sir," Marcus replied serenely. "Traffic at the gate held me up. I circled around as close as I could."

"Excuses again," Bobby grumbled, tugging at his tie until it hung loose. "That is the problem with people these days. No pride, no work ethic."

Marcus said nothing, navigating the car into the line of cars leaving the site.

The silence hung, broken only by the rumble of the motor and an occasional honking horn as cars flowed onto the main road. Bobby couldn't drop it.

"You saw the kind of people coming through those doors. That's the company I keep." His voice held smugness that lingered like perfume. "Leaders. Innovators. People who make history. Not bureaucrats, not complainers. Men and women who get things done."

Marcus maintained his eyes on the highway. He had listened to multiple iterations of this speech many times in the past.

"My family built this company from scratch. Generation after generation, the vision was handed down as a family heirloom. That is how I sit here. It is in my heritage. You people should be thankful to work for a man such as myself."

Marcus's jaw hardened. His fists gripped the wheel a fraction tighter, but he said nothing.

The car hummed onto a wider street, streetlights casting white bursts across Bobby's face. He spoke brusquely, annoyed at the silence. "Are you hearing me at all?"

"Yes, sir," Marcus said.

"Then respond. Do you understand what I'm saying?"

Marcus hesitated, choosing his words. "I see that you are proud of your family, sir."

"Proud?" Bobby snorted. "That doesn't even begin to tell it. I am living proof that vision prevails. Not whining, not begging for the handout, not this incessant chant of entitlement. Vision." He leaned back, pleased, a self-congratulatory smile spreading across his face.

The sedan turned onto the highway, the lanes opened wide, and traffic slowed. Streetlights marked their path in equal intervals, one behind the other.

Bobby's voice grew in anger again. "And one more thing. If people like you stopped complaining so much and started doing, perhaps you would do something worth remembering."

The words struck like stones. Marcus kept his eyes forward, lips sealed.

Bobby edged in closer, his voice cutting through the dark. "Think driving me counts as a contribution? Think drivers are remembered through history? No. History remembers leaders. Men like me."

Marcus's lips parted, but whatever he was going to say, he wriggled back into silence. He pressed his weight harder on the wheel.

Headlights flashed suddenly on the other side of the road. A second vehicle swerved, the driver distracted by the glow of a smartphone screen. Marcus moved in an instant, jerking the wheel to the right to avoid the crash. Tires screeching, the sedan spun on the asphalt. Bobby screamed as the guardrail came up, and then the world exploded into chaos.

The impact came from the driver's side. Metal shrieked as the other car clipped them hard, the sound sharp and violent, like steel tearing apart. The driver's side window shattered instantly, glass bursting inward in a spray of fragments that glittered for a split second before tearing into flesh and upholstery.

The airbag detonated against Marcus's chest with explosive force. The blow knocked the breath from his lungs and snapped his head back against the headrest. White pain burst across his ribs as the seat belt locked tight, bruising muscle and bone. His ears rang violently, a high-pitched whine swallowing every other sound as the sedan spun out of control, tires screaming against asphalt. Marcus tasted blood as the car slammed into the guardrail.

Bobby was not wearing a seat belt, and upon impact, Bobby's body was thrown sideways with brutal momentum. His head struck the window frame, then the glass itself, which shattered inward and rained down into his scalp. Shards embedded along his hairline and temples, instantly opening deep cuts, the dark, heavy blood soaking his collar and running down the leather seat.

His lower body twisted hard as the car rebounded, his spine bending at an unnatural angle. There was a sickening thud as his back struck the door, and then his body collapsed in on itself, limp and unmoving.

The world went white. For a moment, Marcus could hear nothing but shrill ringing in his ears and the hiss of the engine. His chest burned where the airbag had struck him, each breath sharp and shallow. Warm blood trickled from a cut above his eyebrow, stinging as it slid into his eye.

Then instinct cut through the fog.

Afghanistan. Dust in the air. Smoke. A Humvee on its side. A man pinned wrong, blood everywhere. A voice shouting over gunfire—*"Don't move him. Stabilize the spine."*

Marcus forced the driver's door open, metal groaning as it bent. Pain flared through his ribs as he climbed across the console, glass crunching beneath his boots.

Bobby was slumped in the back seat, unconscious. His head was tilted at a dangerous angle. Blood poured freely from his scalp, matting his hair and dripping onto the seat and floor. His breathing was shallow, uneven, a faint rattle accompanying each breath.

"Mr. Phillips," Marcus said, his voice steady despite the fear tightening his chest. He pressed two fingers to Bobby's neck.

A pulse.

Weak. Thready. But there. Marcus stripped off his jacket and pressed it firmly against the head wound, applying direct pressure without lifting—exactly as he had been trained. Blood soaked through almost immediately, but he did not let up.

"Stay with me," he said, more command than plea.

He carefully repositioned Bobby's head, aligning it with his spine, one hand braced at the base of the skull, the other holding pressure on the wound. Bobby groaned faintly, pain rippling through his lower back, his body trying to shift.

"No," Marcus said firmly. "Don't move."

He spoke aloud, grounding himself, inventorying injuries the way muscle memory demanded.

"Airway clear. Breathing shallow. Severe head trauma. Possible spinal injury."

Sirens wailed in the distance. Red and blue lights flickered through the broken windows as emergency vehicles closed in. Marcus stayed exactly where he was, ignoring the pain in his chest, the blood on his hands, the tremor starting in his arms. He did not release pressure. He did not let Bobby move.

Help arrived within minutes. Paramedics swarmed the wreck, moving fast and deliberate. One stabilized Bobby's neck while another replaced Marcus's jacket with sterile gauze and compression bandages. A cervical collar was fitted. Bobby was eased carefully onto a backboard, then onto a stretcher. Oxygen was applied. One of the paramedics looked at Marcus, eyes wide as he took in the blood-soaked jacket, the positioning, the pressure technique.

"You did everything right," he said. "If you hadn't controlled the bleeding and stabilized his spine, he wouldn't have made it. You seem stable, sir, and another ambulance is on its way for you. We need to get him to the hospital. They'll be here in a few minutes, so stay calm."

Marcus nodded once, the adrenaline finally draining from his body. His hands began to shake as he stepped back, ribs throbbing, vision blurring.

The ambulance doors slammed shut and roared into the night, siren screaming.

Marcus leaned against the wrecked sedan, chest heaving, smoke curling around twisted metal and shattered glass. He wiped blood from his face with shaking fingers as he heard the sirens approaching.

He had saved a man who had mocked him minutes earlier. A man who never saw him as anything more than a driver. Duty and empathy had compelled him where pride could not.

In the ambulance, Bobby Phillips slid deeper into unconsciousness. The overhead lights blurred together in lines. Somewhere in the background of the ringing in his head, he could hear a faint clinking of chains in the blackness. He did not know it yet, but the world he had built in presumption and denial had split open. He was moving toward an accounting he could never have imagined.

Chapter 2

Major Warning

The perpetual hum of machinery, interrupted only by the fragmented beep of a heart monitor, filled the hospital room. A tangle of wires and tubes connected Bobby Phillips to machines that were the only things keeping him alive. The monitor lights cast an unhealthy green sheen over his motionless body.

Nurses darted and vanished in gentle efficiency, adjusting IVs, taking vital signs, and writing on tablets. The hospital staff was multicultural: an African American nurse who updated Bobby's chart with careful attention, a Filipino respiratory therapist who tinkered with his ventilator, a Latina aide who cleaned his forehead and arms with loving care, and a young Indian-American resident who double-checked every medication order.

They nursed him with the same dedication they would offer any patient, although grumblings among them spoke of familiarity with who he was. The gala had been covered by the news. Everyone knew the man in the bed was Bobby Phillips, a powerful CEO whose influence stretched into every corner of the media. Some of the staff members had heard his speech, or at least had seen the clips shown on the web. His comments regarding immigrants and "so-called marginalized groups" had already begun riling people. And here he was, at their mercy, his survival resting on the shoulders of the individuals he had ridiculed.

In the waiting area down the hall, Marcus, his chauffeur, sat after being released from the ER with his eye and arm bandaged. His breathing was easier since he had received pain treatment for his bruised chest. His concern was not for himself but the man who had shouted at him mere minutes before the crash.

Demanding news, reporters swarmed the lobby of the hospital. Security kept them back, but rumors were spreading. Was Bobby Phillips dead? Was his empire losing its figurehead?

The machines hummed, steady and unyielding, their rhythm indifferent to Bobby Phillips, the man they sustained. In the stillness, uninvited fragments of memory surfaced, drifting through him with the same cold precision as the fluorescent light above.

He remembered missed birthdays, not because he was away, but because he'd chosen not to come. Candles were extinguished without him. Cakes were cut, wrapped, and placed in refrigerators he never opened. He always sent gifts. Expensive ones. He had convinced himself it was enough. Presence, he told himself, was overrated. Legacy mattered more.

School recitals came back to him in flashes. He recalled watching one through a phone screen, the video muted while he sat in a boardroom discussing quarterly projections. His daughter's face had searched the crowd, then hardened slightly when she did not find him. He remembered thinking she would understand someday. Children always did, once they learned how the world worked.

His son had learned faster. Bobby remembered when the boy stopped arguing with him altogether. Disagreements turned into nods. Opinions turned into silence. Bobby mistook it for maturity, even pride. He told himself he was raising a disciplined young man, one who understood expectations. Only later did he realize the boy had simply learned it was safer not to speak.

At home, conversations shifted when he entered a room. He noticed it but dismissed it. He believed people became careful around authority. *That's respect*, he thought. The quiet meant they were listening.

Clara, his loyal executive assistant, had learned this lesson too. Bobby remembered her standing in his office doorway, file in hand, pausing before speaking. She always adjusted her words, softened truths into suggestions. When she corrected him, she did so carefully, wrapping facts in neutral language, avoiding his temper. Bobby never questioned why. He believed hesitation meant deference. He liked it.

Marcus was the same. The man had once tried to engage him, offering brief comments, occasional observations. Over time, those faded into silence. Bobby filled the space with his own voice, mistaking the absence of response for agreement. It never occurred to him that Marcus had simply stopped believing he would be heard.

Thinking back now, he could see it clearly. The distance had not arrived all at once. It had accumulated slowly, like dust on polished surfaces. A meeting chosen over a school play. A raised voice that silenced a conversation. A dismissal that taught people it was better not to try.

He had surrounded himself with people who complied, not because they respected him, but because they feared the cost of resistance. And he had worn that fear like a badge of honor.

In the hospital bed, stripped of his authority and his voice, Bobby felt the weight of that realization press down on him. He had mistaken obedience for loyalty. Silence for admiration. Isolation for power.

The machines continued their quiet work. Somewhere nearby, nurses spoke in low voices. Bobby remained motionless, but something within him stirred, unsettled. The memories did not accuse him; they did something worse. They revealed him.

Long before the crash, long before the machines, long before the whispers in his room, Bobby Phillips had already been alone.

Inside the darkened room, Bobby's eyelids fluttered, but he did not wake. His body remained still, but in some distant recess of his brain, a creaky door opened.

It began as soft whispers, like leaves rustling on tree branches. Then came a rumble of a growl, like thunder some distance off. Bobby's chest rose and fell more quickly. The heart monitor picked up speed, then leveled out.

He was pulled into a location that was not the hospital ward, not the city, or anything he recognized. His surroundings were initially black, thick, and endless, until a figure emerged.

There was a man—broad-chested, face furrowed like an ancient oak—standing before him. He wore simple clothes, the kind of thing a farmer in the mid-1800s might wear. His eyes, though, were sharp and ablaze with disappointment and fire.

"Bobby," said the man, his deep and unmovable voice steady, "you don't know me, but you carry my blood in your veins. I am your great-grandfather, Samuel Phillips."

Bobby looked around, confused, his pride for the first time in years swept aside by something more akin to fear. "This is a dream. Just a dream."

Samuel shook his head. "No, boy. This is no dream. This is a warning."

Bobby stiffened, trying to regain control. "Warning? Of what? My company is solid. My legacy intact."

Samuel edged closer, his bulk imposing. "You think legacy is money in the bank and your name on the buildings. You think success is written in your blood. But you recall incorrectly. You forget those who carried the weight while you enjoyed the adoration."

"I built everything I have," Bobby asserted. "My father built before me. My grandfather, before him. It is in us. We are visionaries."

Samuel's expression hardened. "You're building chains, Bobby. Chains of indifference, of pride, of blindness, of vanity. Do you feel them bearing down on you?"

Iron weights then materialized on Bobby's chest, clinking as they extended. Each bore an inscription: *Ingenuity and Labor Ignored. Sacrifice Overlooked. Voices Silenced.*

Bobby pulled at the chains. "What is this? Get it off!"

Samuel told him, "This is what you bear. The debt you owe to those you disregard. The workers whose toil built your enterprise. The minorities whose ingenuity, service, and labor made your comforts possible. You live as if they do not exist. And tonight you live because of them. If not for that driver, if not for those doctors, nurses and medical staff, you would already be dead."

Bobby shook his head wildly. "They are doing their jobs. That is all. Nothing more."

Samuel's voice swelled like a storm. "Jobs? They are doing more than jobs. They are keeping this country afloat—the same country you diminish them in. Without them, you would have no riches, no business, no heritage."

The chains dug deeper into Bobby's chest. He staggered. "Stop this!" he yelled.

Samuel's finger pierced the air accusingly. "Three will come to you. Three voices. They will tell you what was, what is, and what yet may be. You will see the truth behind your heedless ways. And if you do not change, if you refuse, you will be lost. Your name will be only shame. Your grandchildren will curse it."

Bobby's haughtiness broke down. His voice faltered. "Why me? Why now?"

"Because I see where you're going, just like me. I see the empty empire you admire, just like I did. And I will no longer let the blood of this family further stain with your pride. You want to know why I won't let you continue down this path?" Samuel's voice cut through the darkness, sharp and raw. "Sit down, boy. It's time you learned the truth of what this family is really built on."

The blackness churned around them. The chains tightened again, pulling Bobby to his knees, and he sat down. He choked for air.

Samuel's voice thundered. "This is your last chance. Pay attention. Listen to me. Learn. Or be damned to a legacy of devastation."

Space shook, and Bobby was falling, chains dragging him down into the darkness of his own fear.

The darkness fell away, and Bobby was in a wide, empty field. Rows of crops extended into the distance, the earth rich and newly turned. A farmhouse, its windows gently aglow with lamplight, stood in the center of the field. There was the smell of dirt and grime, of a life that Bobby had never known.

Samuel Phillips stood at the edge of the field, his boots pressed deep into the soil. The land stretched outward in long, uneven rows, but Bobby could see it now for what it was. The crops were thin. Leaves curled inward. Stalks bent beneath the sun, exhausted and brittle.

"This was not the land you imagined," Samuel said quietly. "It did not prosper because of my strength or my vision. It was dying along with farms all around us."

Bobby followed his gaze. "Then how did you build everything?" he asked. "How did the farm survive?"

Samuel closed his eyes. When he opened them again, there was no pride left in them—only sorrowful memories.

"It survived because I took what did not belong to me."

The air shifted. The soil darkened, rich in some places and barren in others. Samuel motioned forward, and the field reshaped itself. At the edge of the property stood a smaller plot, separated by a rough fence. The crops there thrived. Corn stood tall. Beans climbed their stalks. Squash spread wide leaves across the soil, trapping moisture, protecting the ground.

"There was a family," Samuel said. "Franklin Freeman and his wife and children. Negro sharecroppers on land I considered worthless. I let them work it because I believed nothing would come of it."

Bobby watched as Franklin knelt in the dirt, pressing seeds into the soil with careful hands. Two small children ran nearby, laughing, their feet bare, their joy sharp against the failing land around them.

"I asked him why his crops lived while mine failed," Samuel continued. "He told me about the Three Sisters. Corn, beans, squash. Companion planting. Knowledge he heard passed down from Native Iroquois. Soil preservation. Balance."

Samuel's voice tightened. "He shared it freely. No contract. No demand. He believed helping me would help everyone."

The vision shifted. Bobby saw Samuel copying the method across his own fields. Slowly, yields returned. Neighbors noticed. Whispers followed.

"I realized I possessed something valuable and could sell it to farmers," Samuel said. "Not knowledge I earned. Knowledge I borrowed—no, stole."

The scene darkened. Samuel went into town, explaining the method to other farmers. Money exchanged hands. Praise followed.

"I sold it as my own," Samuel admitted. "I called it insight. Innovation. Business."

Bobby's chest tightened. "But it wasn't."

"No," Samuel said. "And when questions began, when others asked where I learned it, fear took root. So, I spread rumors about the family. They're organizing. They want our land. They're dangerous."

Samuel watched his younger self hearing the rumors spreading like fire and doing nothing.

"I did not strike the match that destroyed," he said. "But I let the firestorm spread. Silence is a powerful accomplice."

One night, torches appeared. A mob gathered in town. The Freeman shack, barely more than boards and prayers, was suddenly engulfed in fire. It burned fast. Too fast.

Bobby felt the scream in his bones before the sound reached his ears. Then there was only fire. And ash.

"Their small children," Samuel said, the words like broken glass. "The girl was three, and the boy was five. They died calling for their parents, who were still working in the fields and came running but were too late. Too late to save them. Too late to do anything but flee for their own lives and were never seen again."

Bobby felt the chains tighten around his chest, pulling him down. He tried to speak but couldn't find air.

"I watched it burn," Samuel continued, relentless. "I stood there and watched what my lies had created. And I said and did nothing. I took that blood money and built an empire on it."

Samuel fell to his knees in the dirt. "I told myself I had not killed them," he said. "That I had merely benefited from circumstances. That lie followed every man in this family after me."

Bobby swallowed hard. "What did you do then?"

Samuel rose slowly. "I ultimately sold the farm. The field dissolved into paper. Deeds. Ledgers. Contracts. I believed leaving would cleanse me. I told my son I had built everything myself."

The vision shifted to town and a newspaper and printing business.

"I carried the same theft with me, after buying several businesses," Samuel said. "Only now it wore cleaner hands. I exploited workers by paying them little wages or none at all. I called it progress."

He turned to Bobby, eyes burning. "That is the lie you inherited."

Samuel stood beside him, boots stamping down into the ground. "This was my land," he said. "Stony ground, but we broke it up. Your great-grandmother and I planted wheat and corn here. Our first crop. We thought we did it all ourselves. But we weren't by ourselves."

Bobby looked down at his neat fingers. "I don't see anyone."

"You will," Samuel said.

And then, abruptly, there were people in the field—women and men bent low, hands pulling weeds, backs bent to the sun. Their faces furrowed, their complexions sun-browned and heritage-darkened. A young Negro man carried a bag heavier than Bobby had ever imagined being lifted.

Bobby frowned. "Who are they? Farmhands?"

"They were everything," said Samuel firmly. "After our farm turned around, I needed help to harvest it. Negro workers labored late into the night to accomplish it."

Bobby smirked, though uncomfortably. "They worked for wages. That's business."

Samuel's gaze narrowed. "Pay? Pennies, if that. Do you know how many nights they returned home with empty stomachs so I could fill my pockets? Do you know how many hands were bruised so I could claim I was a wealthy landowner?

"I did not pass this land down to my son," Samuel said, his voice low. "I sold it. I told myself that leaving it behind would erase what I had done. That if I walked away from the soil, I could leave the guilt buried with it."

He looked out over the field, eyes hollow. "When I spoke to my son later, I told him the success had been earned by our hands alone. That we had built it ourselves. But that was a big lie. The fact is, we constructed it upon their blood and sacrifice."

The photos in the field were altered. Bobby saw a barn under construction. White beams supporting a high, driven home. Next to it stood not just Samuel's family, but neighbors of every kind: Irish immigrants, freed Black men, a Chinese carpenter with steady hands. They constructed the barn in one day, voices blending in song and sweat.

"I let him believe that our prosperity came from vision and grit," Samuel continued. "I did not tell him about Franklin Freeman. I did not tell him about the knowledge I stole, or the family who was destroyed so I could claim success without consequence."

Samuel's jaw tightened. "I thought selling the farm would absolve me. Instead, it only carried the pattern forward."

Samuel's tone mellowed but intensified. "You sit in offices now, padded with wealth, and inform others that they do nothing. But every generation before you was born on the shoulders of people you never speak of. We are alive today because of those you look down on."

Bobby shook his head. "Times have changed."

Samuel stepped forward, his worn face inches from Bobby's. "The times change, but the truth does not. You are blind because you wish to be. Look again."

The mood changed again. Bobby saw an open ledger book on a desk in an office. Pages listed debt, names, and wages. He read them and realized something: many wages had not been paid. Names were scratched out, marked with *credit* or *settled*.

"Is this something?" Bobby asked.

"Remember the story of what we owed and never paid?" Samuel said. "They gave the labor, the knowledge, the brawn, and we gave them scraps. And we said we were self-made. That is the lie you have inherited. That is the lie you spread with every sneer, every dismissal."

Bobby's gut twisted. He wanted to object, but the pictures unsettled him.

Samuel pointed toward the horizon, where darkness lay. "And it didn't end there. When I sold the farm to buy businesses in the city, the same people followed. Negroes, Irish, German, and Chinese immigrants worked for pennies while I sold goods for dollars. You are standing on the shoulders of giants, Bobby. But you behave as if you climbed alone. I told myself distance would bury what I had done. I believed leaving the land behind would silence the memory of the Freeman family and wash the guilt from my hands."

He shook his head slowly. "It did not."

The vision shifted. Smoke rose from factory stacks. Warehouses lined crowded streets.

"The same pattern followed me."

Bobby felt the weight of it settle.

"I told my son I had earned everything on my own," Samuel said quietly. "That lie was easier than the truth. I bought struggling businesses, kept the ones that turned profit, and discarded the rest along with the people who built them. Printing presses came next. Advertising. Ownership of distribution."

The skyline flickered forward in time.

"My son continued it," Samuel said. "He refined it. Learned that controlling information was more powerful than controlling land. From soil to trade, from trade to influence. And you," he said, meeting Bobby's eyes, "perfected it."

Samuel's voice hardened. "You did not climb alone. You never did. You climbed by stepping on people and calling it vision."

Bobby's voice trembled, but pride still lingered. "That was then. They made their choices. Everybody works for somebody."

Samuel's face set like steel. "You're missing the point. Without them, there would have been no choices for us to make. They paved the ground you now wipe your shoe on. And if they had walked out—if they had said no—everything would have collapsed."

The figures in the fields and the businesses began to vanish, their faces dissolving into wisps of smoke. The chains on Bobby's chest tightened once more, the links red hot. He choked.

Samuel leaned close, his voice like thunder across the prairie. "You bear these chains because you refuse to acknowledge. Every link is a debt unpaid, a life unclaimed, a voice stilled by your pride. And they are growing heavier yet."

Bobby knelt, grasping at the burning metal. "I don't want this. I didn't ask for this."

Samuel's eyes flashed with rage. "You didn't ask, but you took. You benefit each day from their labor, their sacrifice. And you spit on them to claim it means nothing."

Samuel stepped forward, close to Bobby's face, and Bobby could see the centuries of regret carved into his features.

"I've been silent for a hundred fifty years," Samuel said softly. "Silence is a choice you make once and then forever pay for. It compounds like interest, growing heavier with each generation that keeps it."

The field darkened, the farmhouse consumed by shadows. Samuel stood alone over Bobby.

"I am telling you this because hope remains," Samuel went on. "But it is not for me to demonstrate to you. There are others who will come. They will reveal that which was concealed, that which exists, and that which is to come. Pay heed to them, lest you be entombed beneath these chains eternally."

The air grew cold. The chains jangled louder. Bobby was being pulled back into the shadows again, Samuel's words echoing in his mind.

"Three voices will arrive. Respect them, or be destroyed by your own ignorance."

And Samuel vanished.

Bobby floated in the vacuum, breathing hard, chest on fire from the weight of the chains. For the first time, fear pierced his arrogance. He had lived a life of confidence in his own superiority, but here, in this foggy no-man's-land between dream and death, he felt the truth encroaching. He was not immortal. He was not a self-made man.

And yet worse, he was not a master.

The emptiness crept closer around Bobby until it was swallowing him whole. No pasture, no farmhouse, no sign of Samuel. Nothing was left but the chains, their metal spitting with a weak light, pinning him down with every labored breath. Each pulled tighter now, forcing against his chest, sinking into his shoulders. He stumbled forward, yet there was nothing to stumble toward.

"Hello?" His echo returned to him, faint and small. "Is anyone there?"

The silence hung. And then there was a sound of metallic clinking, low, like the rubbing of thousands of chains against stone. Bobby turned. Out of the blackness emerged a crowd of humans, faceless, indistinct, but very definitely human. They moved forward in slow procession, burdened by heavy chains of their own. Some carried broken tools; others dragged heavy books. Their lips shaped soundless screams.

Bobby withdrew. "What are you? Back away from me!"

A figure stumbled in his direction, and though its face was still indistinct, Bobby felt its gaze piercing him. A whisper echoed in space, not of a single voice but with many that blended.

"We were forgotten. We were used to it. We were dismissed."

Bobby covered his ears. "No, no, this isn't happening. I don't believe this!"

The chains on his chest tightened in response to his refusal. The crowd's whispers, though muddled, became a boom.

Samuel's voice returned, resonating from above while his shape did not. "These are the lives bound to yours. Every person passed over. Every effort muffled. You carry them whether you think so or not. You forge new chains every time you choose pride over fact."

Bobby collapsed to his knees, gasping. "I didn't know. How could I know?"

"You did not want to know," Samuel thundered. "You shut up voices that spoke the truth to you. You mocked those who sought to remind you. You closed your eyes and believed blindness was power."

The faceless individuals, their chains clanking, moved closer to attack him. Bobby flinched, covering his head, believing they would drag him into their fold.

But instead, they stopped short, backing away into the darkness. The silence grew heavy again. Bobby lifted his head, shuddering.

And Samuel's voice cut through quieter, but more menacing. "You asked what your fate would be if you didn't change? Behold."

The shadows drew apart like curtains, and a glimpse of a city Bobby knew appeared. His city, the one with his company's glass towers shining above the skyline. But here, the towers were in shambles. Windows shattered. Streets were cracked and deserted. Stores closed, their signs askew.

Bobby's breath stopped. "What happened?"

"Without the very people you despise," Samuel said, "this is the world you inherit. The doctors vanished, the engineers vanished, and the workers abandoned ship. You ridiculed and said they didn't matter. Imagine America if they believed you."

Bobby got up and looked out at the empty streets. Trash swirled across the sidewalk. Power cables sagged, black. Factories went dark. The media empire that was his name was a shell.

"No," Bobby gasped. "That won't happen. Things don't finish like that."

"They do," Samuel said, his voice unflinching. "Remove the hands that heal, the brains that build, the spines that labor, and see how fast your world disintegrates. And you—your name, your company, your so-called legacy—they will all rot. Nobody will cry. Nobody will apologize to you. They will spit on your tomb."

Bobby shook his head furiously. "Stop it! Stop showing me this!"

The vision vanished, the blackness snapping shut again. Bobby leaned against the weight of his chains, sweat running down his face. His pride, his armor, now felt flimsy and ridiculous.

"What do I do?" His voice shook, almost childlike. "How do I stop this?"

There was a seemingly endless silence before Samuel's voice came back.

"You listen. You allow yourself to see what you will not see. Three will come. They will not flatter you, they will not deceive you, and they will not allow you to hide. They will show you America's past, its present, and its yet-to-be future. You will have to face it all."

Bobby's heart was pounding. "And if I don't?"

"Then you will be consumed by the very chains that bind you. Your memory will be for naught. Your soul will be merely one more faceless voice in the sea of the overlooked."

The chains that tightly held Bobby's chest released and fell to the ground with a jangling clatter. He gasped like a drowning man breaching the surface of the water.

"Why free me?"

"Because it is not yet too late," Samuel answered. "But it will be soon. Mark this evening, Bobby Phillips. Mark it well. The choice is yours, but the cost of ignorance will be higher than you can pay."

The hollowness began to fold in upon itself, the rush of wind filling his skull. Bobby stumbled about in the darkness, but there was nothing to grasp. He fell backward once again, spinning in darkness, Samuel's final words echoing in his mind.

"Prepare yourself. They are coming."

With a brutal jerk, Bobby's eyes snapped open. The hospital ceiling came into view. The beeping heart monitor, harsh and persistent, filled his ears once again. A nurse hurried to his side and called for the doctor.

Bobby blinked rapidly, sweat trickling down his face. His lips were open, but nothing came out. He still had the shadow of the chains across his chest, their searing weight, the reminder of Samuel's threat.

Talking quietly, the nurse readjusted his IV. Bobby scowled at her, observing that she was the same one who had checked his vitals earlier. A Black woman, probably younger than his own daughter, with a professional demeanor. He recalled Samuel's words: *"Without them, you would already be gone."*

For the first time in years, something inside Bobby Phillips's chest snapped—not arrogance, not control, but fear. True, unbreakable fear.

And somewhere deep inside his mind, a whisper lingered.

"They are coming."

Chapter 3

Great-Grandmother—Voice of America's Past

Bobby stirred in the haze of his coma, though he did not know it. He was not in a hospital bed beneath antiseptic lights and machines, but standing on ground that seemed pulled from his memories and dreams. Fog, rolling low across fields that stretched without end, clung to the earth. There was something in the air he could not explain—a weight as if history itself was pressing upon his chest.

Out of the fog, a woman emerged. She was tall, her back straight despite her age, her hair neatly pinned beneath a modest bonnet. Her long dress and shawl of muted earth tones seemed to belong in another era. Her eyes were sharp, alive with a kind of wisdom Bobby had never respected in life.

"Who are you?" Bobby said, his voice feeble, shaking. "Another ghost? Another lecture?"

The woman's face contorted in a smile-frown. "I am Eleanor Phillips," she said to him. "Your great-grandmother. Tonight, however, I am more than family. I am the voice of the past, and I have waited for you."

Bobby scoffed, though uneasy trembled in his chest. "Another ghost with a lesson to teach me. Do you all think you can shame me into reform?"

Eleanor's gaze did not waver. "Not shame, Bobby. Truth. You will behold what has been hidden from you, what history books buried, what pride destroyed. And then you must decide if you will go on walking blind or open your eyes."

The fog dispersed, and a vision materialized in front of them before Bobby could answer.

He stood in a small workshop. Wooden gears, pendulums, and pieces of metal covered the table. A man bent over the parts, his dark skin glistening with sweat, his hands moving with careful precision.

"Benjamin Banneker," Eleanor whispered. "In the 1750s, he built a fine wood clock, the first of its kind in America, from memory after studying only a pocket watch. He went on to write almanacs that predicted solar eclipses, weather, and tides. Farmers, sailors, and scholars all depended upon his work. He even wrote to Thomas Jefferson, urging him to recognize the hypocrisy of slavery."

The man wound his clock, the mechanism clicking to life and ticking away with precision.

Bobby stared, his brow creased. "A clockmaker? That's what you brought me here to see?"

Eleanor's eyes hardened. "Not just a clockmaker. A scientist, a mathematician, a man who showed genius had no color. When our family was trading slaves and boasting about property, Banneker was building knowledge that fed the nation. And you never knew his name."

The workshop disappeared, making room for the creak of a millstone. Another man, older, stooped to hand-crank a device, the corn kernels dropping into fine meal beneath his invention.

"George Peake," Eleanor spoke. "A free Negro man in the 1790s. He invented the hand mill for grinding corn, an invention that spared families hours of backbreaking labor. His invention spread from farm to kitchen across America."

Bobby sniffed. "So he built a kitchen tool. You're saying that changed America?"

Eleanor's eyes narrowed. "Every meal your ancestors ate relied on work like this. Every harvest that filled their tables was sustained by tools made by men like Peake. Without him, families starved. Do not call survival insignificant."

The scene shifted again. Bobby now stood in a tailor's shop. A man with confident eyes squatted over a cloth while mixing strange solutions in glass jars. He immersed the fabric, scrubbed, then revealed the restored and intact cloth.

"This is Thomas Jennings," said Eleanor. "In the 1820s, he patented dry scouring, the first technique of dry cleaning. He was the first Negro to be granted a US patent. He used the money he earned to fund abolitionist causes and freedom suits."

Jennings straightened, looking past Bobby as if daring him to dismiss his accomplishment.

Bobby folded his arms. "Dry cleaning. That's business."

"Business that turned into revolution," Eleanor corrected him. "He put his profits into fighting slavery, into freeing others. What have you put your profits into, Bobby? Yachts? Banquet dinners? You mocked men like Jennings, but his efforts yielded not only clothes but justice."

The tailor's shop dissolved into fields. There were furrows of earth in every direction. A man guided a strange wooden device pulled by a mule, which planted seeds at regular intervals into the earth.

"Henry Blair," Eleanor whispered. "He was alive in the 1830s. He invented the corn planter and the cotton planter, which made planting faster, easier, and less backbreaking. He was only the second Negro to receive a US patent. And he could not read or write, but his mind saw what others could not."

The seeds fell in rhythmic rows, full of the promise of harvest.

Bobby shifted restlessly. "Machines like that are everywhere now. He was just . . . early."

Eleanor's voice grew stern. "And still, no one taught you his name. Your textbooks lauded Eli Whitney and his cotton gin, but they omitted Blair. They omitted Jennings. They omitted Banneker.

They remembered your ancestors and called them pioneers, while they erased men who fed, clothed, and sustained the nation."

The fields vanished. There was mist around them again. Bobby was silent, his chest tight.

Eleanor turned to him. "These were the hands that laid the foundation. Negroes were not just enslaved laborers, as your history reads. They were innovators, inventors, scientists, and thinkers. And whenever they created, the nation grew stronger. And yet, men like you claim you built your fortunes alone."

Bobby's lips curled into a sneer, but they faltered halfway. "So they made some tools. Some machines. You're saying America wouldn't exist without them?"

Eleanor stepped ahead, her voice level and low. "Yes. Were it not for them, you'd have no food on your plate, coat on your back, crop in your field, or the science to predict the weather. Without them, you'd have no America to boast of."

Bobby turned away, his jaw set. The fog came again, dense and damp against his chest. He wanted to protest, to laugh, to tell her it was an exaggeration. But he could still hear the tick of the clock in Banneker's shop, the cornmeal falling through Peake's mill, the hiss of Jennings's chemicals, and the muted thud of Blair's planter. Each sound pulsed like a heartbeat, one that he had not formerly heard.

Eleanor's voice cut through the mist. "You will hear more. Much more. And with each name, each invention, each sacrifice, the chains you have forged for yourself out of ignorance will clank louder until you will no longer be able to ignore them."

Bobby made no reply. His silence was not agreement, but for the first time, it was not denial either.

The fog spun around them again, enveloping Bobby and Eleanor as though they stood in a huge hallway. Light glinted on the walls, and scenes opened like windows. Each scene radiated with its own life, a theater for history he'd never heard.

"Look close, Bobby," Eleanor said. "These are the hands you never thanked. The minds you never named."

The first window depicted a tiny 1870s town. Smoke billowed from a wooden building, fire encasing the second story. A Negro man with resolute eyes dashed toward it, flinging open a folding ladder that locked into place in front of the fire.

"Joseph Winters," Eleanor explained. "He patented the fire escape ladder. Before him, families trapped in upper stories had no way out but to leap into the streets. His invention saved lives in towns across the country."

The vision shifted, showing frightened families climbing down to safety. Bobby rubbed the back of his neck. "Ladders? That's . . . practical, sure, but hardly revolutionary."

Eleanor's eyes were sharp. "Tell that to the children who made it to the next day."

A second action played out. A clean elevator shuddered upwards inside a hotel, its door closing neatly and solidly without anyone touching it. The creator who designed it stood proudly next to the mechanism.

"Alexander Miles, a Negro inventor," Eleanor said. "He automated elevator doors in the 1880s. Doors were opened accidentally, and men fell to their deaths. His invention is utilized in every skyscraper you've ever entered."

Bobby's mouth opened, then closed. He considered the elevators in his own headquarters—smooth, automatic, seamless. He had never wondered who designed them to be safe.

The corridor brightened, and now a bearded fellow, hunched over a desk filled with wires and devices, pressed a key, and messages clicked across a telegraph machine. On the other side of the tracks, another machine clicked back. A train barely managed to screech to a halt, missing a collision.

"Granville Woods," replied Eleanor. "The Negro Edison. He invented the telegraph system for railroads in the 1880s. Trains would have continued crashing into one another if he hadn't been around. He gave America safe travel and sped up communication."

Bobby stared at the immobilized train, his heart pounding against his will.

The fog carried him through a hot field where an old man in tattered rags was standing before a group of farmers. He pulled peanuts, showing how they fertilized the land, then switch-planted corn and sweet potatoes.

"George Washington Carver," Eleanor spoke softly. "He saved the Southern farm. He taught farmers how to restore depleted soil, how to grow crops that nourished millions, and how to reduce dependence on cotton. His data was gold."

Bobby fidgeted. He had heard the name before, but only as a symbol, a passing mention in a book. To actually see the man among white farmers who clung to his advice unsettled him.

Then there was a man attempting to wear a bizarre mask tied over his head as he charged into a smoky corridor. He emerged coughing but otherwise intact, removing the mask to reveal a device that had purified the air. Later, he stood at an intersection, grasping a small replica of a three-position traffic light.

"Garrett Morgan," Eleanor said. "In the 1910s, he created the gas mask that saved soldiers on the battlefield and firefighters at home. In the 1920s, he created the yellow caution signal for the traffic light that keeps all the intersections in your city moving in a regular pattern. He made safety an invention."

The vision clung to Morgan's determined face. Bobby's throat dried.

Another inventor entered a tiny workshop and delicately adjusted gears within a car engine. "Richard Spikes," Eleanor described. "He changed cars with his automatic gear shift in the 1930s. His innovations made car travel safer and more productive, shaping the automobiles in which our family traveled so proudly."

The gears clicked into place, a car gliding smoothly down a street. Bobby scowled, uneasy.

Visions came on with a quicker speed now. Planes roared overhead, the shiny bombers of the 1940s. With them flew escort fighters, tiny ones, piloted by Negro men whose piloting ability dispelled every racist epithet thrown at them.

"The Tuskegee Airmen," Eleanor stated proudly. "The very first Negro pilots to fly in combat. They flew with integrity, escorting bombers with unprecedented records. They dispelled the lies that indicated Black men were too dumb or too cowardly to fly. They flew over 1,500 combat missions. Although a significant number of American bombers were shot down during World War II, not a single bomber was lost while being protected by the Tuskegee Airmen."

Immaculate in its alignment, the plane banked in the air. Bobby could not mock this time. His teeth gritted as he imagined men such as these being forgotten with his ancestors, flaunting courage.

The atmosphere shifted once again. In a clinical laboratory, a white-garbed man analyzed vials of blood. Shelves behind him were lined with rows of jars.

"Dr. Charles Drew, a Negro physician," Eleanor said. "He invented techniques for separating and storing blood plasma, the first large-scale blood banks. Thousands of soldiers lived because of him. All transfusions today are founded on his genius."

The blood bank glowed like a cathedral of redemption. Bobby's throat tightened as he swallowed hard.

Trucks rumbled past in the area, each with refrigeration equipment on board. Inside, food and medicine stayed fresh after miles of travel.

"Frederick McKinley Jones, a Negro inventor," Eleanor said. "His refrigeration process revolutionized truck transportation. Without him, food spoiled sooner, medicine became ineffective, and people's lives were shorter. With him, America thrived."

The image flickered, and now a Black couple stood beside a monitor. A screen cast the first closed-circuit television broadcast, grainy but clear.

"Mary Van Brittan Brown and her husband Albert," she said. "They created the first home security system in the 1960s. All the cameras in all the businesses and homes today are the result of their patent."

The vision sped up, showing houses in blocks where cameras deterred crime as they watched stores. Bobby's heart raced.

Finally, a Black woman leaned over and scribbled equations on a blackboard. Figures and equations went on and on, the math of satellites and orbits.

"Gladys Mae West," Eleanor answered. "Her mathematical models and calculations created the foundation of the GPS. All the navigation systems, all the gadgets that guide planes, boats, and your own car are indebted to her brilliance. You'd be lost if it weren't for her contributions."

Bobby stood frozen in place. He had yelled at Marcus more than once for taking "the wrong turn," relying on his GPS as gospel. To think of it, the work of a Black woman absent from his education made him uncomfortable to his very core.

The hall darkened, visions closing in succession. Eleanor got up and stood before him, her voice heavy. "Do you see now? These aren't footnotes. These are pillars. They hold America upright. Without them, your empire collapses before you even begin."

Bobby's sneer failed him. His lips parted, but the words clogged in his throat. He wanted to wave it away, call it a bluff. But he still saw Morgan's mask, Drew's blood banks, and West's equations. They haunted his mind like specters that would not leave.

Eleanor's voice softened. "You have mocked the very people who gave you safety, health, and freedom. You thought your name was full of history. History does not remember arrogance. History remembers those who have saved lives."

Bobby turned aside, jaws clenched, chest heavy. He could not utter a word. Silence was stronger than denial.

The mist curled around once more, ready to push him further into truth.

As the fog rolled, Bobby felt the hallway dissolve into open air. He and Eleanor stood upon a ridge overlooking rivers, fields, and forests that stretched as far as one could see. The land pulsed with life, and its beauty was mixed with unseen wisdom.

Eleanor's hand went up. "Before our people came and claimed this land as their own, it was sustained by nations who already had the knowledge of how to survive on it. Native peoples. Their knowledge sustained not only themselves, but the new people as well, who would have died without it."

The vision shifted. Bobby saw women and children toiling over hills of earth. Corn stalks reached for the sun, beans twirled around their stakes, and spreading squash leaves blanketed the earth. Water flowed through small canals excavated by hand, irrigating the plants with precision.

"This," Eleanor explained, "is the Three Sisters—corn, beans, and squash—all together, grown with advanced irrigation. A system as scientific as any your farms use today. Before there were European settlers on this continent, Native farmers had created sustainable food systems."

Bobby looked at the mounds, the soil dark, the plants sturdy. He swallowed hard. "I . . . I didn't learn this. Not like this."

"No," said Eleanor. "Because to teach it would be to admit that survival in America had been made possible by Indigenous knowledge."

The vision changed again. Soldiers crouched in trenches, the chaos of World War I surrounding them. Between the thunder of guns, Bobby heard voices talking in Choctaw—rapid, spasmodic. The message was relayed, unbroken by the ears of the enemy.

The Choctaw Code Talkers, Eleanor responded. "Their code was an unbreakable language that saved lives in World War I."

The work moved to the Pacific theater of World War II. Navajo Marines spoke into radios, their voices unintelligible to foes but crystal clear to friends.

"And the Navajo Code Talkers of World War II," Eleanor continued. "Their voices were victors. Wars could have been lost, lives wasted without them."

Bobby's heart pounded. The weight of their unheralded effort fell upon him.

The vision shifted once more. Native healers pounded willow bark into a powder, forcing it into a soldier's hand. Another spread a salve of bruised plants on sunburned skin.

"They gave the world medicine," Eleanor stated. "Painkillers, the first syringes made of bone and bladder, and even sunscreens made from plants. You pop aspirin and use lotion today without ever knowing whose brains came up with them first."

Bobby's fists were clenched. He was prepared to debate, but the words were stuck in his throat.

The mist swirled, and the aroma of spices and rich food hung in the air. Bobby stood in a bustling kitchen where women and men rolled out dough, stirred massive pots, and carried hot platters. In the background, hard-hatted men poured concrete, laid railroads, and lifted steel beams.

"Latinos and Mexican Americans," she stated, her voice steadfast. "They bowed their backs in fields, making harvests. They laid railroads and highways. They nourished cities and brought light to the world."

A doctor came over, a machine in his hand. "Domingo Liotta, an Argentine surgeon," Eleanor continued. "He created the first effective total artificial heart to be implanted in a human being in the 1960s."

The heart pumped in the patient's chest, the machine keeping him alive.

A young professor stood in front of a chalkboard, drawing diagrams of seismic waves. "Arturo Arias Suarez, a Latin American inventor," Eleanor went on. "He invented Arias intensity, a measurement of ground motion and earthquake strength, in the 1970s, saving lives through preparation."

Next was a young man, smiling as computer code scrolled on a screen while facing a chalkboard. "Luis von Ahn, a Guatemalan-American," Eleanor said. "He co-created CAPTCHA and reCAPTCHA in the early 2000s. He gave the internet a way to tell the difference between humans and machines."

In the background, a man strode with an incubator into a country clinic. A premature infant breathed rhythmically within. "Claudio Castillón Lévano, a Latin American engineer," Eleanor declared. "He invented the portable incubator and respirator for premature infants. Thousands of children were saved through his invention."

The kitchen and building areas returned with laughter and sweat. Eleanor's voice remained haunting. "Latinos gave you, life, security, culture, and innovation. But their names, too, were forgotten."

The vision shifted once more to a team of railroad workers. Bobby saw Asian men hammer spikes into the ground, their eyes rimmed with exhaustion. Theirs was labor that carved routes through mountains, binding a continent together.

"Chinese, Irish, and German immigrants, as well as Native Americans and freed Black people, built the bulk of your railroads," Eleanor said. "The work was often very dangerous, and the wages were low. America moved forward on their backs."

The vision became clear. A man in a lab coat held a mask, the fibers thin and intricate. "Dr. Peter Tsai, a Taiwanese American scientist," Eleanor said to him. "He created the filtration system for the N95 mask in the 1990s. His work saved millions when the pandemic struck."

Another flash came. A woman in a lab traced sequences of DNA. "Flossie Wong-Staal," Eleanor said. "She is a Chinese-American virologist and molecular biologist. She was the first scientist to clone HIV, which helped prove that HIV is the cause of AIDS."

Next, a man plugged a small device into a computer. "Ajay Bhatt, an Indian American computer architect," Eleanor said. "He co-invented the Universal Serial Bus (USB). Every flash drive, every port you've ever used carries his signature."

Then, two young men uploaded a video onto a simple platform. "Steven Chen and Jawed Karim," Eleanor said. "They founded YouTube. They reshaped how the world communicates."

The visions shifted again, and a young man stood with a slim music player in his hand. "Anthony Fadell," Eleanor stated. "Lebanese American, he led the team that designed the iPod. He transformed the way you hold music, the way you think of memory itself."

And finally, Eleanor placed a steaming cup in Bobby's hands. "And coffee," she breathed. "It began in Yemen, propagating from the Arab world to fuel industries and nations. Even your morning routines are not your own."

Trembling, Bobby's hand closed around the cup. His eyes leapt from fields to railroads, from the incubator in the hospital to the GPS formulas still fresh in his mind. His mouth parted. "All of this. All of them. And I did not know."

Eleanor stepped closer. "Forgetting is what makes the powerful relax. But forgetting does not annihilate truth. It annihilates gratitude alone."

Bobby's voice cracked. "Why did they not instruct me in this?"

Eleanor's expression softened. "Because to learn it would mean having to respect those you excluded. And respect would involve humility."

The visions faded, the fog rising again in tendrils. Bobby was silent, his pride withering piece by piece. Stronger than denial, uncertainty for the first time set deep roots within him.

Chapter 4

The Hidden Struggles of the Past

The fog lifted, but this time the air was heavy. Heat hugged Bobby's skin with an acrid odor of sweat, dirt, and iron. He blinked, trying to adjust, then stopped.

Stretching out before him were cotton fields, white and seemingly boundless in the sunlight. Dark faces of men and women were bent over rows, their red hands raw from ripping fibers that clung to bleeding palms. Men on horseback yelled curses, their whips cracking back and forth with a sound that made Bobby's stomach turn.

Eleanor stood beside him, her face somber. "This is the beginning of most of America's wealth. You see the fields, the crops, the labor, but not the cost. Millions of Africans were taken from their families, chained together, and sold into bondage. Generations lived and died in servitude, their backs bent so others could gain a profit."

Bobby's throat closed when he watched a young woman fall under the weight of a heavy pack. An overseer's whip cracked across her back, and her scream filled the air. Bobby stepped back, repelled.

"This . . . this was centuries ago," he blurted in his tight voice. "It has nothing to do with me."

Eleanor's eyes grew tight. "Doesn't it? The cotton enriched the North's textile mills. It fueled foreign trade, built banks, financed railroads, and lined coffers. Wealth was multiplied on the backs of the slaves. Our family, like so many others, inherited profits from that system. You sit on land fertilized by their blood."

Bobby shook this off, shivering. He tried to recall his old defenses, but the slaves' screams cut through him. He saw a small child holding on to her mother's hand, her bare dusty feet, her eyes too wise for her years.

"Stop showing me this," he growled.

"You have to see," Eleanor continued. "Unless you know the cost, you cannot know the truth."

The fields of cotton were replaced by obscurity, and instead was the seemingly infinite stretch of the Great Plains. Grassy hills curved into the distance, but Bobby instantly perceived the difference—soldiers in line, rifles glinting in the sunlight. Before them were Native men, women, and children with their scant possessions. Their faces furrowed with a combination of fear and resolve.

"This was their land," Eleanor breathed. "Native tribes lived, farmed the land, hunted, and settled here for centuries. But with the white settlers pushing westward, treaties were signed and repeatedly broken. Promises of peace, of land, of living together, all broken for greed."

Bobby watched soldiers push the families in front of them onto a narrow path that sliced through the endless wilds. The children clung to their mothers' legs, the elderly fell and stumbled, and the line continued and continued.

"Trail of Tears," Eleanor panted. "Thousands of Cherokee, Choctaw, Creek, Chickasaw, and Seminole men, women, and children were forced to march hundreds of miles. With disease, starvation, and exposure, thousands died. Their homes were stolen, their graves left behind, their culture trampled under the boots of expansion."

Bobby's chest ached as he watched a boy tumble onto the road, his father racing toward him with shaking arms. The soldiers shouted, pushing the line forward.

"This is progress?" Eleanor insisted. "This is the glory you boast of? To build a country on stolen land, to kill the people who originally lived there, to write treaties with ink and then burn them for gain?"

Bobby shut his eyes and shook his head. "It was another era. Folks didn't think the same way. That's the way the world operated."

Eleanor's answer was swift. "Convenient alibis for brutality. They thought enough to write proclamations of freedom and liberty. They thought enough to claim justice for themselves. But when it came to others, they chose profit, not humanity. That was not ignorance—it was greed."

The trail dissolved into mist, and the screams of the repressed dwindled from sight. Bobby's eyes snapped open, his heart racing. He wanted to protest, to reject the past, but the visions lingered in his mind—the lash slicing on flesh, the empty eyes of forcibly removed children, the sound of broken promises. His resistance felt less firm now, even though he clung on in desperation.

"It's not fair to judge history by today's standards," he snarled.

Eleanor looked at him, her voice cold but firm. "And still, history judged them too. All the lashes, all the broken treaties, all the killings left a mark. You can ignore it, but the fact never disappears. It is there, and it demands to be heard."

The fog began to swirl again, pulling Bobby into the next vision.

The fog lifted again, and Bobby found himself on hard-packed earth. The atmosphere was dry, burning his nostrils, and the horizon stretched out to infinity beneath a scorching sun. It resembled a small desert town at first glance, but then he noticed the fences. Long rows of barbed wire hemmed in wooden barracks, their roofs sloping, their windows boarded with thin slats. Guard towers loomed over the corners, manned by soldiers armed with rifles.

"What? Where?" Bobby said, his voice confused.

Eleanor's face folded. "This is America in the 1940s. This is where the internment camps are. More than one hundred thousand Japanese Americans, two-thirds of them naturalized citizens born here, were removed from their homes, their businesses, and their communities following Pearl Harbor. Their offense was their heritage."

Bobby observed the scene. There were groups of families in front of the barracks, their suitcases filled with the little they owned. Children kicked dust as they tried to play while warily eyeing the guards. The elderly sat with downcast faces, their eyes lowered. A young man in his early twenties, trying to keep his younger brother from crying, grasped a baseball glove and flung a grimy ball high into the air.

"They look like prisoners," Bobby complained.

"They were," Eleanor replied. "They were stripped of their rights, their dignity, and their livelihoods. Farms were lost, businesses shut down, homes seized. Generations carried the wounds of being told they did not belong in the land they worked so hard to create."

Bobby shook his head, trying to understand. "America was at war. There was fear of spies."

Eleanor's voice cut through the balmy air. "Not a single act of sabotage was ever proven amongst them. Racism was invoked as a pretext for fear. These citizens were scapegoats, and their sons fought and died for the same country that locked up their families."

The view shifted a little, and Bobby was looking at soldiers in tidy uniforms. Their patches read: *442nd Regimental Combat Team.* Resolve on their faces, young Japanese American men marched in lines.

"They volunteered to fight in Europe because their families were incarcerated," Eleanor explained. "They were one of the most decorated units in American history. They died fighting for freedoms their parents and siblings didn't have."

Bobby's chest felt heavy. He could catch their eyes, not bitter but with a still strength that unsettled him. They were men who had good reasons to turn their backs on America, and yet they gave their lives for it.

"Why would they do that?" he whispered.

"Because they still held out hope for America," answered Eleanor. "A hope that has been too often disillusioned, but it still clung to the hearts of those who were kept from its protection."

The scene dissolved into another place. Bobby was in a small schoolroom with kids sitting at worn desks. They had old books, some of them with missing pages. There was a Latina teacher with tired eyes writing on a chalkboard as she worriedly glanced at the doorway, where a suited man stood clutching a clipboard.

"Segregated schools," Eleanor told him. "Minority children herded into underfinanced classrooms, denied resources, and informed they were not deserving of better. This took place centuries after slavery, centuries after treaties, centuries after promises of equality. This was not history. It is nearer to your own life than you realize."

Bobby scowled as the children traded pencils, one stub passed hand to hand. A little boy raised his hand to answer, his face glowing with pride, but the teacher hesitated, glancing again at the man beside the door. When the boy butchered a word, the man smiled and made a note.

"This is wrong," Bobby burst out before he could stop himself.

Eleanor gazed at him. "Yes, it is. And yet generation after generation endured it. Segregation in housing, medical treatment, schools, transportation, and even burial grounds. Do you still believe it's all behind us?"

Bobby's fists were balled. He wished to say yes, to demand that the world had changed, but the faces of suffering closed in so near. The accumulated sum of their tales, stacked on top of each other, destroyed his certainty.

"Those are horrid pages," he growled. "But they are not my fault. They are not me."

Eleanor stepped forward, her presence stern and unyielding. "Nay, this is the very chain you are forging. Denying to see, turning away from the past as another's, disregarding the debt as not affecting you. With every refusal, another link is forged. And too tightly bound, you will never be able to break it."

The barracks, the soldiers, the classrooms—they all dissolved into shadow. Bobby felt the weight of history pressing down upon him, weighing in on his lungs, so he couldn't quite breathe.

The haze settled once more into the vision of tidy suburban boulevards. Ranks of neat houses sat in the light of the afternoon, their lawns cut, their windows sparkling with pride. But Bobby observed a little too closely. One block was filled with life—children on bicycles, mothers talking, fathers cutting lawns—while on the other side of the railroad tracks, the homes slumped with age. Their siding had peeling paint, and broken windows were covered with cardboard. The streets were cracked and unpaved.

"This is segregation in housing," Eleanor stated. "Redlining, decades of policy and zoning that branded entire neighborhoods off-limits due to the people who lived there. Banks wouldn't lend money to families of color, no matter how hard they worked, how much they saved. The wealth of generations was stolen not by mistake, but by design."

Bobby saw two men carrying clipboards in business suits, knocking door to door on the bad side of town. There was a young Black couple standing on their porch, clutching a bundle of papers. Hope and frustration were etched on their faces. The men shook their heads, and the couple's shoulders dropped.

"You mean they couldn't even buy houses?" Bobby whispered.

"They could give it a try," Eleanor replied. "But whites alone received the finest loans, and whites alone resided in the finest neighborhoods. Property values rose on one side of town and fell on the other. That carried over generation after generation, leaving some rich, some poor. You boast about building success, but do you not realize how much of it was luck?"

Before Bobby could react, the scene shifted once more. He found himself in a hospital ward now. The walls were filthy, the machinery outdated. A mother was on a cot with her feverish child using a folded newspaper to fan herself. Doctors rushed by, harried, and a nurse fought to get along with evidently inadequate supplies.

"This is health care for so many minorities," Eleanor said. "Segregated hospitals, under-staffed clinics, no access to life-saving treatment. Black and brown families were sent to other wings or denied services outright. Children died of treatable illnesses. Mothers died in childbirth. All while more well-off communities had the best medical care at their fingertips."

Bobby swallowed hard as he watched the mother's eyes, pleading and desperate, as she asked the nurse to help her. The nurse could only shake her head, pools of tears welling.

Bobby gasped. "This is unacceptable."

Eleanor's eyes did not blink. "It was reality. And its shadow still lingers. Do you think inequalities in health, education, housing, and labor ceased to exist in one night? They resonate forward, shaping lives today."

The ward yielded to a schoolroom, then to a waiting room for buses, with partitions separating the waiting rooms, then to a dinner with a sign above the door that read: *Whites Only*. Each picture flashed in sequence, a rapid fire of exclusions, humiliations, and slammed doors. Bobby's heart pounded as the load settled on him.

Finally, the visions ceased. Eleanor towered over him, her demeanor maternal but firm.

"You see the struggles. You see the resilience. And yet you still tell yourself it is all in the past. That is your comfort. That is your shield." Her eyes burned with silent fury. "But comfort does not erase the chains. Denial does not free you. You are bound because you are prospering from what others endured, and you mock the very people who cleared the way beneath your feet that you now walk upon."

Bobby looked away, his voice cracking. "What do you want me to do? I can't make what happened before I was born different."

"You can't change the past," Eleanor said sharply. "But you can change what you choose to acknowledge, what you choose to celebrate, and what you choose to heal. Until you do, the chains will remain. And they'll drag you under."

The vision stilled.

For the first time since she appeared, Eleanor looked away.

The heat receded. The screams faded. The world narrowed to just the two of them, standing in a quiet space that felt almost like a parlor, dimly lit and heavy with dust. Eleanor's hands trembled slightly at her sides.

"You think I showed you these things to accuse strangers," she said softly. "But I am not finished telling you the truth."

Bobby shifted uneasily. "You already have."

"No," Eleanor replied. "I've told you what America did. I have not told you what we did.

She met his eyes now, and the disappointment there was sharper than anger.

"When Samuel told me what his success was built on, he did not confess out of strength. He confessed because the guilt finally broke him. And when he did, he begged me to tell our son.

Bobby's breath caught. "You didn't."

Eleanor nodded once. "I didn't want to, but we did."

The silence stretched.

"I told myself it was for stability," she continued. "For safety. For reputation. I told myself that truth would destroy everything our family had built. And perhaps it would have."

Her voice hardened. "But silence destroyed something far worse."

The room shifted again, subtly. Bobby saw a younger Eleanor standing beside a sickbed, Samuel pale and shaking. He saw her pleading. Saw her son standing rigid, refusing to accept it.

"He said it would ruin the family," Eleanor whispered. "That the business would collapse. That people would come for what we had. And I chose comfort over courage."

Bobby swallowed. "You protected the family."

"I protected the lie," she corrected. "And I taught the next generation how to do the same.

Her gaze bore into him now. "You learned silence from us," Eleanor said. "You learned how to look away, how to justify, how to tell yourself that success excuses harm. You didn't invent that arrogance. You inherited it."

Bobby's fists clenched. "I didn't know."

"And that," Eleanor said, her voice breaking just slightly, "is exactly what we told ourselves."

The images returned briefly, but this time smaller. Samuel signing papers. Businesses changing hands. Printing presses rolling. Newspapers stacked high.

"We convinced ourselves that as long as we didn't speak of it, it no longer belonged to us," Eleanor said. "That time would cleanse what truth could not."

She shook her head slowly. "Time only buried it deeper."

Bobby felt something shift inside his chest, a pressure different than fear. He remembered moments he had dismissed: Clara pausing before speaking. His children going quiet in rooms when he entered. Marcus absorbing words meant for wounding.

Silence, learned. Silence, inherited.

Eleanor stepped closer. "You are not condemned because of what Samuel did," she said. "You are condemned only if you repeat him. Only if you choose comfort again."

Her voice softened, but the weight of it did not. "I stayed silent because I was afraid," Eleanor said. "You stay silent because you believe you are entitled not to listen. That is the difference. And that is why this burden is now yours."

The room darkened at the edges. "You still have a choice," Eleanor said. "But understand this: Every generation that refuses truth does not escape it. It simply passes it down, heavier, sharper, harder to carry."

Bobby felt the chains again, not tightening but hanging.

"And if you fail," Eleanor said quietly, "it will not be because history trapped you. It will be because you chose not to see."

The fog thickened once more, drawing him toward the next vision.

The fog crept up again, curling thick and oppressive over the houses, the hospitals, the faces. Bobby felt his knees go weak as the pull of those intangible chains strained at him. He longed to wake, shake it off, and return to the heat of his old life. But something inside him knew that this was only the beginning.

The quiet lengthened, marked by Eleanor's final words before the dream faded away.

"History ain't over. It is in you, surrounding you, fashioning every breath you draw. The issue isn't whether you'll confront it, but whether you'll continue to pretend it did not occur."

Chapter 5

Former College and Early Partner
—Voice of America's Present

The fog swirled again, colder this time, and Bobby was pulled through it like a stream taking him under the water. When it cleared, he found himself in a familiar setting—a college campus, but decades younger than he remembered it when he had last walked there. Red-brick buildings towered above him, and the ring of students' laughter drifted across the quad.

He turned around, confused. "What is this? Why am I here?"

Behind him was a voice, quiet but tinged with disappointment. "Because this is where you started forgetting who you were."

Bobby whirled. A big man with broad shoulders and a friendly face and eyes that held warmth along with judgment stood before him.

Bobby was struck with a moment of recognition. "David?" he asked. "David Wright?"

The man nodded once. "Your roommate. Your partner. The one you put aside when my ideas got in the way of your profits."

Memories poured in. There were nights spent late in their dorm room making plans on napkins, dreaming up ways to drag Phillips Media into the future. David had been the driver, bringing together a team with new ideas, platforms, new readers, and more intelligent ways of linking them together. Together, they'd created mock-ups for Bobby's family company, one slide at a time, a promise of what could be.

On the day of the big presentation, Bobby arrived without David. Bobby stole David's name from the product, appropriated the ideas for himself, and won the accolades. The money, promotion, and fame were all attributed to Bobby. David was given nothing but betrayal.

At that point, Bobby had justified it readily. Why should David get to share in the heritage? David's family did things with their hands, blue collar through and through. Bobby was born to the business, heir to the throne. In his mind, David should have felt fortunate to even be given a place in the room.

They had not spoken for years.

The scene shifted again.

Time moved forward in uneven steps. The college quad dissolved into a cramped office space above a laundromat, the air faintly scented with detergent and burnt coffee. The windows rattled whenever the machines below spun too hard. Folding tables had been pushed together to form desks. Secondhand chairs bore mismatched scuffs and stains. A whiteboard leaned against the wall, crowded with arrows, timelines, revenue models, and ideas written in several distinct handwriting styles.

David stood there, younger, thinner, but alive with purpose. His sleeves were rolled up, tie discarded, hair perpetually uncombed. Around him were the people Bobby had never met: a Black software engineer hunched over a laptop, fingers flying as lines of code scrolled; a Latina marketing strategist standing barefoot on a chair to sketch campaign ideas higher on the board; an Asian American logistics analyst recalculating distribution paths across a city map taped to the wall. They argued. They laughed. They stayed late.

"We weren't pretending," David said. "We weren't chasing trends. We were building something we believed in."

Bobby watched the nights stretch long. Pizza boxes were stacked in corners. Coffee cups multiplied. The whiteboard filled, erased, and filled again. A logo was taped crookedly to the wall, debated fiercely, replaced, then taped back up with a laugh.

"We didn't have your money," David continued. "But we had ideas. We had range. We had people who understood audiences your company never bothered to speak to."

The image sharpened. Proposals were printed clean and professional. Financials tightened. Metrics highlighted. Each page proofread twice.

"We knew your board," David said. "We knew your reputation. But I thought . . ." He paused. "I thought knowing you would mean something."

The room shifted.

A boardroom. Glass table. Leather chairs. Younger faces, sharper suits. Bobby at the head, fingers drumming, eyes flicking to his phone. David stood alone at the end of the table. His partners waited just outside the door, quiet, hopeful, listening for cues.

Bobby heard his own voice now, distant but unmistakable. "Too risky. Unproven leadership, not aligned with our brand or values."

No questions. No discussion. No request to see the work. The meeting ended before it began.

The rejection letter arrived next. Polite. Brief. Final.

"You didn't even pretend to consider us," David said softly. "You had already decided who we were before we spoke."

The vision returned to the office above the laundromat.

The whiteboard was still full, but the energy had thinned. One partner sat staring at a phone, refreshing email. Another quietly boxed up personal items. The engineer closed his laptop slowly, like someone shutting a door for good.

"We waited," David said. "Weeks. Then months."

Bills stacked on the desk. Rent notices slid under the door. A calendar crossed into another season.

"They didn't leave because the idea failed," David said. "They left because hope costs time. And time costs money."

The lights flicked off one by one.

"I kept telling myself you'd call," David continued. "That you'd say you made a mistake. That you'd at least ask a question."

Bobby saw David alone now, sitting at the folding table, proposal still open in front of him. The logo peeled slightly from the wall.

"But you didn't," David said. "And that's when I understood." He turned to Bobby, his expression steady, resolved. "It wasn't just business," he said. "It was the realization that no matter how good we were, the door was never meant to open."

David met Bobby's eyes. "That's why I stopped calling," he said. "Not because I was angry. Anger still hopes." He paused. "I stopped because I saw you clearly."

The office dissolved completely.

"You didn't lose me," David said. "You told me, without words, that I never mattered."

Silence followed.

Not the kind that waits to be broken.

The kind that remains.

"This is not true," Bobby said, shaking his head in denial. "You're just some specter brought to life by my guilty conscience."

"Call me anything you like," David replied, closing the distance between them. "I am the voice of America today. I am here to make you realize what you refuse to acknowledge."

Before Bobby could answer, the campus receded into a blur. When the world coalesced again, they found themselves amidst a bustling hospital. Doctors and nurses hurried past, treating patients in overcrowded wards. Bobby noticed the diversity immediately: Black surgeons consulting with Asian American anesthesiologists, Latino nurses escorting patients, and a South Asian resident studying charts attentively.

"Look around you," David told him. "This is America today. Hospitals run on the skill and dedication of people of every background. You talk of vision and leadership, but without these hands, these minds, the system collapses."

Bobby watched as a surgeon adjusted a ventilator for a child struggling to breathe. Another doctor was about to perform emergency surgery. A nurse comforted a frightened patient in Spanish, her voice soothing.

"They're just doing their job," Bobby complained in weakness.

"Jobs that save lives," David snapped back. "You brushed off efforts as though they didn't mean anything, and these individuals carry the nation on their backs day in, day out. Would you have lived through your accident without them?"

Bobby remained silent. He shifted uneasily as the hospital fell away to be replaced by a classroom.

Rows of kids sat at their desks, computers in front of them, while a teacher guided them through a lesson. Bobby watched children of every hue—Asian, Black, Latino, white—leaning forward with interest. Across the room stood an African American teacher, her voice soothing, weaving together history and science in a cycle that made the students' faces glow.

"Education," David said. "Shaping the future. Teachers of color make up one-third of the teacher force, and they often tutor students who live outside a system created with them in mind. They fight underfunding, overcrowded classrooms, and erasure, and yet they teach."

Bobby's gaze lingered on an eager young girl who raised her hand. Her braids bounced as she talked, her face alight with confidence. He thought of his own daughter, now estranged, and something in him ached.

The classroom dissolved, reshaping itself into a military base. Soldiers in line, boots hammering the floor in unison. Bobby's eyes widened in shock as he gazed at their faces. African American, Asian American, Hispanic, Latino, and Native American men and women soldiers in line, uniforms crisp, posture rigid.

"These are your country's warriors," David answered. "They fight wars that you fund from the comfort of your boardroom. They bleed on far, distant lands, even when they return home to a country that treats them less. Look closely, Bobby. Officers and soldiers of every color and gender stand here, giving everything for a nation that often gives them so little in return."

Bobby's chest tightened as the command tone reverberated. He watched as a young Latina soldier, her expression stern, marched by with an overpacked duffel. He recalled his own empty words praising "our troops" without ever really knowing who those troops were.

The scenery shifted again, this time to a rolling countryside. Fields of crops stretched along the horizon. Women and men bent low, tending vegetables in the scorching sun. Their garments were tattered, their hands hard, their bodies exhausted.

"Farms," David continued. "Dinner on your plate, profit in your corporations. Who picks it? Who labors in the heat and cold? Migrant workers, immigrants, and minorities who will do the jobs others won't. They keep the system running, but they live in poverty."

Bobby felt perspiration bead on his forehead. He had been served lavish dinners, gourmet cuisine, every bite brought by this labor he never considered.

David's tone became bitter. "This is America, Bobby. Not the boardrooms you love, not the functions where you boast. The hospitals, the classrooms, the farms, the bases. Sustained each day by people you disregard. Do you still want to tell them they don't give much?"

Bobby's jaw dropped, but the words caught. His usual arrogance deserted him, overcome by a tightness in his throat he couldn't shake.

The fields dissolved, and he was once more standing in the mist. David's outline remained there, immovable and steadfast.

"This is merely the beginning," David said. "You have yet to see the trials. You will now."

Bobby's stomach churned. He wanted to turn and leave, to awaken, but the fascination of the vision pulled him in. He remained steadfast as the mist grew dense again.

The fog rolled back in, and Bobby's feet touched pavement. He was standing on a street corner in a dark place at night. There was a distant wailing siren. Red and blue lights flashed, and his heart pounded.

A young Black man with his hands raised wore a look of panic on his face. Two officers bellowing orders, guns pointed. The man was trembling, fear etched on every tense muscle of his body. He was probably a bit older than Bobby's son.

"Why are they pulling him over?" Bobby breathed.

David's voice was low, commanding. "Because of his color. Because of assumptions. Because he fits some 'profile.' This is racial profiling, Bobby. It happens every day."

Bobby winced as officers shouted louder, pushing the man against the wall to pat him down. His pockets were empty. Yet, they laughed as if he did something that could not be seen. The man's mother appeared, her voice shaking as she begged them to leave him in peace. They pushed her aside.

"This is wrong," Bobby muttered under his breath, his stomach churning.

And yet it happens," David added. "This is what you call 'law and order.' This is what you're defending when you mock those who protest. You gaze upon angry mobs. I see families begging that their sons not be next."

The lights went dim, and the street retreated into an office cubicle. A Latina woman typed frantically at a desk. There was a tower of papers beside her. She wore a headset, her eyes tired but resolute.

"This is pay inequality," David explained. "She does the same job as the guy beside her, yet she ends up taking home less money.

Her skin color, her femininity, her accent—all excuses to justify why she gets pennies while they get dollars."

Bobby glanced around. There was a white male co-worker three cubicles away, feet on his desk, earning more money for doing less. He remembered his own company's payroll charts, the unspoken decisions he had signed off on, never questioning why some workers earned less.

The office turned into a waiting room. Families leaned in chairs, their faces pale with sleeplessness. A mother swaddled her child tightly, who coughed harshly, but the receptionist shook her head at the mention of insurance.

"Healthcare disparity," David said. "Minorities tend to be uninsured, refused treatment, and die of preventable illnesses. They work jobs without benefits, live in communities without hospitals, and when they finally get the opportunity to get medical help, they're turned away."

Bobby's throat went dry at the mother's entreaty. The receptionist handed her a stack of forms, her voice flat. Breaking the hush, the cough of the child vibrated through the room.

"You were seen by a doctor who didn't waste time," David told her. "But few get that chance. They're sent to wait, to demonstrate they deserve to be treated, as time expires."

The hospital vanished. Bobby found himself in a school gymnasium among kids. Murals once covered the walls but were painted over with blank beige paint. The bookshelves were half full. Teachers scurried through lessons with old texts.

"Efforts to erase culture," David spoke quietly. "Language programs get cut. History reinterpreted. Heritage suppressed. Children are being shielded from true history. They are being pushed to forget their roots so they can fit into something that was never meant for them."

Bobby watched a young Native boy clasp a book written in his tribe's language to his chest. A teacher removed it from him, saying it was not "approved." The eyes of the boy dimmed as the book was cast aside.

Bobby shifted uncomfortably. He had often ridiculed talk of "representation" and "inclusion," calling it something that was a distraction. But here, with the seriousness on that child's face, it did not feel like a joke anymore.

"Do you get it?" David asked. "They give, they maintain, they create. And yet they get underpaid, over-policed, underserved, erased. The system appropriates their work but doesn't recognize their value."

Bobby clenched his fists as he searched for something to argue. "That's . . . that's not true of everybody. Some achieve. Some get big."

David's gaze was unflinching. "Some do ascend, yes. But theirs is a steeper ascent, the rungs weaker, the ladder shorter. Being successful doesn't end the struggle. You use exceptions to show the system is fair, without note of the millions thwarted by that same system."

The photographs spun once again. The cubicle, the hospital, and the school disappeared. Bobby found himself again trembling in the fog. His chest burdened him, not with material shackles this time but with the weight of knowledge pressing down.

"I don't want to see any more," he whispered.

David's face hardened. "You don't want to, but you must. This is your world, Bobby. This is the America you refuse to see. And you profit from it every day."

The fog hummed, lighter now, demanding Bobby's attention.

David's voice boomed. "There is one more thing you need to see. Someone you know. Someone you've taken advantage of. And someone who illustrates how blind you've been."

Bobby exhaled in short, shallow breaths. He was stiff as the fog began to clear once more.

The fog thinned again, and Bobby found himself in a place that was far too familiar. He saw paths of cubicles, the whine of the servers, and the glass screens that overlooked the city. This was his company.

"Where am I?" Bobby blustered, attempting to sound assertive over the tremble in his voice.

Calm but unyielding, David stood by his shoulder. "Because this is the heart of your kingdom, and because within these walls is one you need to meet."

Bobby's stomach turned over. He had always thought of this building as his shrine to himself, his genius. Now, to stand in it as a ghostly observer, it was hollow.

They passed by the office. Employees slumped over their desks, pecking away at their computers, muttering softly to one another like people do when they're fearful of being overheard. Bobby saw diversity for the first time—Latina analysts, Black engineers, Asian American designers, immigrants answering phones in the call center.

"They are the ones who build what you take credit for," David said.

Bobby frowned. "I hired them. I pay them."

"You take advantage of them," David said. "And none more so than her." He nodded toward a small desk at the back. A woman sat there, dark hair pulled back into a tight bun, fingers clacking over the keyboard, papers precariously balanced on her desk. Her face was tired, but her eyes were bright and full of intelligence.

"Rosa," Bobby breathed, a spark of recognition.

Rosa Alvarez. He had remembered her name from quarterly meetings. She had been with the company for nearly a decade, always quiet, never looking for publicity. He had once called her "support staff."

David's words were restrained but cutting. "She is the woman who developed the prototype that powers your company's most profitable software. She developed it, tested it, and tuned it. And you signed on it."

Bobby bristled. "That's not accurate. I set direction. I gave the resources."

"You took credit," David said with conviction. "You gave her a modest bonus, and to the board, you attributed her work to your vision. She continues to work two jobs to help her family. She rides the bus home from work at midnight, then gets up before the sun rises to take care of her children. And you benefit from her genius."

The office dissolved into a tiny apartment with thin walls and hand-me-down furniture. Rosa entered, her shoulders sagging with exhaustion. Two children darted to greet her, their faces aglow. She hugged them tightly, her smile genuine in spite of exhaustion.

Bobby lingered, his dry throat. Rosa put leftovers onto the table, ensuring her children had eaten before she had a bite. Later, when they were in bed, she sat at the kitchen table with bills in front of her. She massaged her temples, calculating, redoing numbers, trying to stretch her paycheck to cover bills and groceries.

"She's better than that," David asserted. "But you never did get to see her. Not really. To you, she was a name on a spreadsheet, a machine part. You grew rich off her invention, and she was counting pennies to keep the lights on."

Bobby wanted to turn away, but his eyes stayed fastened on Rosa's tired face.

The environment shifted once more. Huddled in a thin coat, Rosa stood at a bus stop early in the morning. The bus ran behind schedule, and she shivered with the cold. Other workers stood nearby—immigrants, single mothers, men, and women who would soon scatter to restaurants, warehouses, hospitals, and offices.

"This is the America you don't see," David said. "These people carry the weight of America every day. They labor while you brag. They make sacrifices while you accumulate, and if they fade away, your empire crashes down."

Bobby's chest ached. "I didn't know," he whispered.

"You did not wish to know," David asserted. His voice was low but firm. "You chose blindness because it was easiest. You tell yourself you are self-made, but the reality is staring you in the face."

Rosa's shape broke apart, fading away into mist. Bobby's hand reached out involuntarily, shaking. "Wait," he breathed. "Let me talk to her. Let me tell her . . ." His voice faltered. He had no clue what he'd say.

David stepped closer, his eyes resolute. "It is not *her* you have to hear it from. It is *you*. You must accept the reality of what you have witnessed tonight. There are Rosas all over the world. Oppressed souls that you never noticed. They are not anomalies. They are the foundation. And you overlook them."

The defenses of Bobby started to crumble more. His voice shook. "What do you want from me?"

"See and recall," David spoke softly. "For if you continue to deny it, the price will come due. And it will cost more than you can imagine."

The fog rolled again, sweeping them out of the apartment, the bus stop, the faces Bobby could not forget.

David's voice rang out as the shadows came up again. "You can no longer play dumb. You have seen the now. The question is whether you will embrace it—or if you will fall."

The fog rolled in again, and Bobby was left shivering, his head reeling with Rosa's tired smile and the burden of her unsung brilliance.

Chapter 6

A Community Gathering

The air shifted, and Bobby blinked. The glistening towers and antiseptic hospitals of the former vision were gone. He was standing on the sidewalk of a neighborhood. Storefronts bore brightly colored murals—painted faces of heroes, workers, and scientists. He caught glimpses of slogans in English and Spanish stenciled over images of clasped hands and open books.

Beside him, his old college roommate appeared, his hands shoved into his jacket pockets. "This," he said, "is where you'll see what keeps America alive today."

They entered through the front doors of a brick building. A hand-painted sign above the door read: *Community Cultural Center.* Inside was a buzz of voices, children's giggles, and the far-off sound of a guitar being strummed. Posters of events lined the walls— heritage nights, food drives, and after-school activities. One of the hallways was filled with framed photographs of local teachers and veterans. The building had a lingering aroma of coffee and tamales.

Bobby's lip curled. "Doesn't look like much."

"Not everything that's important sparkles," the roommate replied.

They entered a large room with folding chairs and round tables. Children sat cross-legged on a rug as an elder stood before them. His long gray braid fell over one shoulder, and his worn hands waved as he talked. A circle of parents and volunteers watched in silence.

The old man's voice was strong, a heavy drumbeat. "Corn, beans, and squash," he said, scooping up tiny gourds from a wicker basket at his feet. "Our people called them the Three Sisters. Each prefers to grow surrounded by the others. The corn stalks rise high and give the beans a stalk to climb on. The beans reach into the soil with energy for next year. Squash spreads wide leaves that keep the ground moist. Together, they keep each other alive."

A boy raised his hand. "So they're like family?"

The elder smiled. "Yes, like family. When the settlers came, they did not know how to survive here. Our people showed them. Without these crops, there would be no harvest, no colonies, no America."

Bobby shifted, folding his arms. "Crops? We're really talking about beans and corn again?"

The roommate nodded to him. "Without those crops, our families wouldn't even have had a table to sit and eat from, Bobby. Without irrigation, they wouldn't have had the farms they bragged about."

Bobby gritted his teeth. He disliked the way the children's eyes sparked at the remark from the elder as they drank in a story that didn't exist in his own textbooks.

The old man finished, laying down the basket. "Don't forget, kids. America didn't sprout up overnight. It was constructed by hands that knew this soil, by lessons learned long before borders were drawn."

There was applause around the room. Bobby remained quiet.

The children parted, and now a uniformed man slowly rose from his chair. He was silver-haired and had a slouching back, but his medals reflected on his chest. He held a cane and leaned on it as he stood before the children.

"My father was Choctaw," he began, his voice deep and raspy. "He used our language as a code during the Great War. The enemy could not decipher it. Lives were saved. Later, during the Second World War, Navajo Marines did the same thing. They called them the Code Talkers. Battles would have been lost without them. Soldiers would not have come back."

He stood there, tapping the cane softly on the ground. "Don't forget this. Our language was once considered worthless. Savage. Then, when war came, it was priceless. Don't let anyone convince you that your heritage is worthless."

The children clapped, and a few of the parents wiped tears from their eyes.

Bobby smiled wryly. "That's all drama. An entire war based on a few words?"

The roommate turned sharply to him. "Not words. Knowledge. Courage. Tactics. You disdain what you do not know, but these voices wrote history. Without them, you'd be speaking German or Japanese today."

Bobby fumed but said nothing. The veteran had already sat down, warmly welcomed by a group of teens who helped him back to his chair.

As the children split off into smaller groups, Bobby walked along the wall. He stopped in front of a large mural of scenes with workers building railroads, fields of crops disappearing into the horizon, and white-garbed nurses wheeling trays of blood stored in bags. The bold letters above the mural spelled out: *We Built This Too*.

A small girl, not more than ten years old, approached him as she pressed a small notebook in her hand. "Are you here to learn about our heroes?" she spoke shyly.

Bobby blinked at her. "Heroes?"

She nodded enthusiastically, opening her notebook to display a drawing of a man sporting a pilot's cap alongside a red plane. "This is a Tuskegee Airman. My teacher informed me that they were the initial Black pilots in the war. They were so good that even when other soldiers lacked trust in them, they saved bombers from being shot down. My grandpa told me they proved everyone wrong." Her eyes shone with pride.

Bobby swallowed, surprised. "That's . . . nice," he stammered.

The girl grinned and ran off to join her friends.

The roommate shook his head, glaring at him. "You see what this place does? It teaches what schools neglect. These kids will grow up being conscious of the names and sacrifices their nation tried to delete."

Agitated, Bobby played with his cufflinks. He didn't want to think about it, to pay attention to the elder's fields, the veteran's code, or the little girl's drawing. But the mural's words seemed to mock him: *We Built This Too.*

He wondered for the first time if maybe, just maybe, the foundations he was so sure were his own legacy had been built on soil that had been tilled by hands he never acknowledged.

The children broke up into workshops. Some huddled around tables with paintbrushes, and others followed volunteers to smaller rooms for individual tutoring. The center hall transformed as chairs were pushed into a circle. Bobby was led to an empty seat, his roommate watching him closely as if daring him to get up.

A woman in her forties, dressed in a cardigan and with the calm smile of a teacher, stood first. Her voice bore the confidence of someone accustomed to being in charge of a room full of students. "I teach history a block away," she said, nodding at a cluster of kids who waved at her proudly. "I tell my students that we stand on the shoulders of those who made this country function, even when they were denied their humanity."

She stood holding a photo of a solemn Black man in a white lab coat. "My grandfather used to tell me about Dr. Charles Drew. He created modern methods of saving blood plasma and built the first blood banks. Because of him, World War II soldiers lived through wounds that would have otherwise been fatal. Even now, every transfusion given in this hospital chain uses his techniques."

She addressed Bobby but did not know his name. "My children ask me why they never hear him mentioned in books. I say, 'History has a tendency to cover up the people it owes the most.'"

Bobby looked away. His throat closed, but he disguised it as a snort. "Doctors, teachers, inventors . . . everyone wants to be in the limelight, I guess."

The teacher shunned him and sat back down.

Next, a man with calloused hands and a reflective vest stood. He smelled faintly of sawdust and paint, the marks of long hours on construction sites. "I work in civil engineering," he said. "My father came here from Mexico. He poured concrete for freeways and laid steel beams in half this city. People like him built the bones of America. And do you know what my cousin tells me now? That our people didn't just work with sweat—we worked with ideas too."

He pulled out a scrap of paper from his pocket with a screenshot printed on it. They were warped letters from a CAPTCHA form. "And Luis von Ahn, a Guatemalan scientist. He created this system. You've all seen it. Type the letters, prove you're human. His work digitized millions of old books at the same time."

Bobby frowned, tilting his head. "You're saying . . . typing squiggly letters saved books?"

The man grinned. "Right. Millions of them. People worked, and history was salvaged. That's contribution."

Bobby said nothing, but his eyes narrowed as though he were tallying.

A nurse then took her turn. She was petite, but her energy filled the circle. She had clean scrubs, but her eyes were tired, the sort of fatigue that you get when you've spent too many nights at too many bedside rails. "I was on the front lines during the pandemic," she said flatly. "We lost people. Too many. But we also saved lives. And I owe that, in part, to Dr. Peter Tsai."

She produced a folded N95 mask from her pocket. "He was a Taiwanese American scientist. He invented the filtering mechanism that allows this to happen. Millions of lives were saved because of it. My patients lived because of him."

Her voice softened, but the gravity of her words pressed down on the room. "Sometimes people think immigrants only bring workers. They forget that we also bring brilliance."

The room buzzed in agreement. Bobby fiddled with his cufflinks, displaying a small twitch of irritation. He wanted to shoo her off, but the mask in her hand was too tangible, too real.

From somewhere around the circle, a teenage girl spoke aloud. She wore a sweatshirt with the logo of her school emblazoned on it, still carrying her backpack slung over one shoulder. "My mother works two jobs," she said. "One in a warehouse, one at home. She says I must learn computers because Latinos are changing too."

She pulled out her phone and pressed the screen, showing a YouTube clip. "Steven Chen and Jawed Karim—they created this site. Without them, I wouldn't be learning guitar, makeup tutorials, or viewing videos from my cousins across the world."

She looked at Bobby curiously, having no clue who he was. "They changed how the world shares stories. That means something."

The room contracted. Bobby's chest tightened. He wanted to roll his eyes, but he caught his roommate's eye and stayed silent.

Then a grandfather stood, grasping his cane firmly. His words were seasoned with Spanish cadences. "I lost my brother as a young child," he stated. "He was premature. Back then, we didn't have anything to keep him alive. Years afterward, a man from Peru, Claudio Castillón Lévano, designed a portable incubator for fragile infants. Now, those babies survive."

He fell silent, his eyes welling up. "I think about my brother every time I see a healthy child. I think of what kind of life we might have had."

There was silence in the room, burdened by his grief.

Bobby fidgeted uncomfortably. He was struck by their words, not because he knew they were true but because he understood how much the stories meant to these people. Their pride was something he could not buy, something his galas and headlines had never been able to offer.

Finally, the instructor spoke again, her voice gentle but firm. "All the tales we recount here are proof that greatness is not owned by a name or a family. It is born in all people, all generations."

The circle clapped softly. Some reached out to clasp hands across the distance. Children leaned against their parents. There was warmth in the circle, a sense of belonging that pushed against Bobby's chest like heartache.

He broke the silence with a snarl. "If these people were as important as you say they are, wouldn't they already be famous?"

Smiling sadly, the teacher looked at him. "Recognition is not value. Truths are hidden because they are harmful to pride. But hidden truths do still save lives."

The circle burst into whispers. Bobby sat stiffly, his arms crossed. But within him, a crack was forming.

The circle of chairs broke apart, and people migrated into smaller groups again. Some of them gathered around tables laden with food—tamales, frybread, collard greens, dumplings—a buffet of traditions side by side. Kids ran, laughing between the tables, while parents scolded and smiled in equal measure. Music drifted in from the corner, where a young man strummed a guitar and an elder rapped out a beat on a hand drum.

Bobby, hands folded behind him, remained stiff beside the railing as he watched. He had moved through hundreds of galas and banquets, all of them shrouded in white tablecloths and shining crystal, but never one where individuals appeared . . . full. Not wealthy, not powerful, but full in a manner he could not measure.

"Come," his roommate urged. "There is something else you need to see."

He led him through a short corridor, the walls of which were lined with black-and-white photos. Soldiers in military gear glared out of them, their names set in neat plaques at the bottom. Women in head coverings and work clothes stood next to them, some holding babies, some holding flags.

At the far wall, a larger display was to come. A memorial board featured dozens of names on small brass plates. Some had stars next to them. Inscribed in bold letters above the display were the words: *For Those Who Served and Were Forgotten.*

Bobby screwed up his eyes. "What is this?"

A man with closely cropped hair and wide shoulders moved forward. His jacket had a patch for a local group of veterans. "This wall commemorates those from our community who served in wars," he stated. "African Americans, Latinos, Native Americans, immigrants. Many returned home to no welcome, no acknowledgment. Some didn't return at all."

He indicated a section close to the top. "See that? Navajo Code Talkers. Their voices were battles. See that line? Black soldiers who returned from Europe and were still told they could not sit at a lunch counter. Here are the Japanese Americans who signed up while their families were sitting in the camps. All the names on this wall bore this country, but most of them were never seen."

The weight of the silence fell on Bobby's shoulders. He fidgeted, eyes darting back and forth across the wall.

At the edge of his vision, a young woman in a white blouse interrupted him, her daughter clinging tentatively to her side. "I tell my girl about Gladys West," she said. "She was a Black mathematician who was born in Virginia. Her work was vital to the development of GPS. If it weren't for her, no one would be able to navigate."

She smiled down at her daughter. "Every day, she taps on that phone, and it tells her where to go. And I tell her, 'That was from somebody who looked just like you.'"

Her daughter smiled, holding up her itty-bitty phone case for her to see.

Bobby jolted, a lightning sharpness stinging him. He remembered growling at Marcus in the car. *"Can't you just follow the GPS?"* He had taken it as gospel, and yet he had never known the mind that came up with it. Now, seeing this mother's beaming face, he felt something churn in his stomach.

The group moved back to the main hall. The food was out now, the plates stacked high with flavors from every continent. Kids stood in line with paper plates and cradled them with open, hopeful eyes. The guitar and drum were joined by a violin, and people began singing a common folk song in three languages at once.

Bobby hovered at the edge, watching. He watched the old vet with the grizzled hair laugh with teenagers, the teacher handing out bread to a nurse, the worker entertaining children as though he were a performer. Each person who was here today was both a thread of history and a stitch in the here-and-now.

His roommate slid into the room alongside him. "Do you feel the difference now? You spend your days in towers and boardrooms, where people fear you and avoid you. But here—here is heart. Here is solidarity. They have more power here than you wield in your entire empire."

Bobby ground his teeth. He wanted to sneer, to call it sentimental nonsense. But he could not avoid the cutting feeling of jealousy.

These people had something he could never buy with all his money: belongings.

The former teacher rose once more and spoke above the music. "Tonight, we honor what has been passed down to us from our people, and what we pass to our children. We don't wait for boardrooms or textbooks to provide us with recognition. We seize it for ourselves. And no matter how many people try to erase our names, we will not be forgotten."

Applause sounded like a wave over the room. Bobby did not stir, his arms folded. Pride in their tones annoyed him, as if the ground beneath him was shifting.

His roommate turned to him. "What are you thinking?"

Bobby released a hasty breath. "I think"—he paused as he hunted for words—"if they tried harder, they'd be noticed."

A silence fell in his chest despite the music and laughter continuing around him. He knew the words were hollow even as they left his mouth. But he clung to them, clung to the pride that had always protected him.

His roommate shook his head, a look of disappointment on his face. "Recognition is not about working harder, Bobby. It's about who gets to tell the story. Tonight, you've heard the stories. Whether you want to admit it or not, they'll stick with you."

Bobby looked away, his eyes gazing down the hall where children had painted *We Built This Too*.

For the first time, the words didn't hurt as if they were an accusation. They rang as truth. And truth didn't sit well with him.

Chapter 7

His Adult Son—Voice of America Yet to Come

The walls of the community center dissolved like mist, and Bobby was left in the middle of an empty street. The gray air was heavy with dust. Streetlights flashed but cast no steady light, and the quiet was broken only by distant shouts echoing off glass towers.

Out of the mist came a form. Bobby's heart skipped as he recognized the shape—broad shoulders, dark eyes, jaw set in stone. It was his son, but not the boy Bobby knew. This was a man now—older, harsher, face neither warm nor knowing. He stood in a black suit, but not a fashionable one. It looked more like a funeral suit, its cuffs worn through with use.

"Daniel?" Bobby gasped.

The figure did not answer. His eyes locked on Bobby, and for the first time, Bobby felt the sharp edge of being sized up and found lacking.

"Speak to me," Bobby ordered. "Are you the guide they told me would come?"

The figure gave one nod. His voice, when he answered, was low, nearly hollow. "I am the voice of what will be. The voice of America Yet to Come."

Bobby tried to laugh, but his throat clamped shut. "You don't frighten me. I've seen visions and ghosts. I know how you do this. Show me what you wish, and let me get back to living."

His son held up his hand. "You will see, Father. And you will regret not heeding earlier."

The air about them shimmered. The towers dissolved into lines of fields, but the earth was dead, cracked like a dried-over wound. The earth fell apart in Bobby's hands when he bent. It was dry, dead, and would not yield.

His son's voice rang out. "Without the ingenuity and inventions of those long forgotten and unrecognized, the soil died. Without them, the crops withered. America's breadbasket is barren today."

Bobby's head shook. "That's absurd. Farmers can adjust. Technology can do anything."

His son looked at him. "Without knowledge passed down, there would be no technology. Only failure."

They walked on, and Bobby found himself walking into what was supposed to be a bustling city. Cranes, rusted and idle, towered over half-constructed highways. Concrete was split open, metal rebar sticking out like bones in a tomb. Bridges collapsed where workers had left their stations.

"No highways," Daniel said. "No bridges. No sweat of the men and women who built this country's spine. The immigrant hands that paved highways, raised steel, laid rail—all gone. You promised you could do without them. This is the America you insisted on."

Screams echoed. Down the street, there was a crowd assembled, red-faced and furious, their chants echoing, "Go back to your country! Go back to your country!" But when Bobby walked up, he found the streets were empty. The crowd was yelling at nothing, their fury waving into the air.

Daniel's eyes glittered. "They screamed until the words were spent. And when the crowd had vanished, so had their gifts. The crowd had believed in victory through exclusion. In return, they left with nothing but absence."

Bobby's stomach churned. He retreated as the crowd screamed louder, their wrath turned back upon themselves.

The scene shifted again. They were on a city street. Skyscrapers loomed overhead, but their lobbies were shut. Bobby tried to force through one of the glass doors, but it would not move. He looked closely and saw the problem: there were no automatic doors to the elevators. The staircases went up hundreds of feet, but nobody was going to walk up them. Office floors were empty because that device had never been invented.

Traffic screeched in the distance. Bobby turned around and took a breath as he looked at the chaos of an intersection. Dozens of vehicles jammed the streets, horns blaring, drivers screaming. Ambulances were stranded, unable to move forward. At its center, lights dangled but offered no guidance, and green snapped to red without warning, leaving drivers slamming their brakes or crashing into one another.

His son said, "Without the invention of the yellow caution signal, the warning that lets drivers slow down and prepare to stop, cities choke. Order turns into disaster."

Bobby swallowed hard, sweat breaking across his temples. He thought of his own vehicle, his luxury car gliding easily through intersections. He thought of yelling at Marcus for being late. Without this invention, there was only congestion and rage.

The odor came next. It was rot, heavy, and foul. A row of trucks clogged along the street, their contents overflowing onto the sidewalk: spoiled meat, curdled milk, melted boxes of medicine. All useless. Rats ran over the mounds.

His son's voice was merciless. "Another lost invention gave trucks refrigeration, enabling food and medicine to be shipped. If it weren't for this invention, modern food distribution systems would not exist. You can imagine our choices and medicines would be limited. This is what comes of our forgetfulness."

Bobby gagged, covering his mouth with his hand. He glared at his son, his voice cracking. "Enough. I understand. It is atrocious. But this is exaggeration. America cannot break apart like this."

His son stepped forward, his shadow stretching out. "You always believed you built by yourself. You always said others could be replaced. But remove them, and your world is destroyed."

Bobby's knees trembled. The chant of the mob trailed behind him, the smell of rot stuck to the air, and looming above it all were the quiet skyscrapers, vacant, out of reach.

His son's eyes glazed over him. "This is only the beginning. You'll see more. You'll see all that you spurned stripped away. And then you'll see what's left of your name."

Daniel did not move forward with the vision right away. The ruined city around them remained frozen, smoke hanging in the air without drifting, broken glass suspended mid-fall. Even the wind seemed to hold its breath.

"For all the things you think you lost," Daniel said calmly, "there were things you took long before this."

Bobby shifted his weight. His voice came out defensive, automatic. "I gave you everything."

Daniel nodded once, slowly. "You gave us expectations."

The street dissolved. They were standing inside a house Bobby recognized instantly. Their old living room. Large, pristine, echoing. Furniture arranged perfectly, as it was never meant to be used. No family photos on the walls. No mess. No warmth. The silence pressed in like pressure.

"When we were kids," Daniel said, "there was only one language spoken in this house."

The room was filled with movement. A younger Bobby paced back and forth, sleeves rolled up, watch glinting as he checked the time. His voice echoed, clipped and precise.

"Be the best. No excuses. Second place is failure."

Daniel watched himself and his sister sitting stiffly on the couch, knees together, backs straight. Not relaxed. Never relaxed.

"You didn't say it once," Daniel continued. "You said it every day. At breakfast. In the car. After school. Before bed. You called it motivation. But it was pressure without rest."

The scene sharpened. A dinner table. Homework spread out.

Bobby leaned over, pointing at a math problem. "Why isn't this perfect? You rushed. You can do better."

"You didn't ask if we were tired," Daniel said. "Or scared. Or confused. You corrected tone. Posture. Pace. Even how we celebrated."

Bobby watched himself interrupt laughter, redirect joy into performance.

"Winning wasn't encouragement," Daniel said. "It was survival."

The image shifted again. A report card was held in small hands. An A-minus was circled in red.

Bobby scoffed. Shook his head. "So close," his younger voice said. "Almost doesn't count."

Daniel's chest tightened as he watched it. "That was the day I learned effort didn't matter. Only results."

The room shifted.

Daniel stood near the doorway with a group of kids, backpacks slung low, voices overlapping with excitement. Bobby entered, surveyed them once, and frowned.

"You hang around people like this," Bobby said, "you'll end up like them."

Daniel's voice was steady now, practiced. "You hated my friends. You called them unfocused. Lazy. Not winners. You said diversity was an excuse people used when they couldn't compete."

The image flickered. Bobby scoffed at names, mocked ambitions that didn't fit his mold.

"You told me if I didn't change," Daniel said, "I'd be just another disappointment."

The house darkened. They stood in a hallway now. Raised voices leaked from behind a closed door. Bobby's voice, sharp and cutting. His mother's voice, quieter, tired, trying.

"That's why Mom left," Daniel said. "Not because she was weak. Because living here meant never being enough."

The door cracked open. Bobby saw his wife standing rigid, arms crossed, eyes dull from exhaustion.

"You didn't hear encouragement," Daniel said. "You heard yelling. Belittling. Criticism dressed up as honesty. Love turned into a scoreboard."

The moment froze on Bobby walking past her, phone in hand, already distracted.

"No one wanted to be around you," Daniel said quietly. "Because nothing was ever positive. Nothing was ever finished. Nothing was ever good enough."

The house was emptied. Furniture faded. Walls dissolved. Only silence remained.

"I didn't rebel," Daniel said. "I didn't scream. I didn't fight. I learned faster than you realized."

Bobby looked at him.

"I learned silence was safer," Daniel continued. "That speaking only gave you something to correct. That disappearing hurt less than being measured." He paused, then added, softer, heavier, "So I stopped needing you."

The future city began bleeding back into view, broken streets replacing the hollow home.

Daniel took a step back. "You taught me how to compete," he said. "How to win. How to judge. How to survive pressure." His eyes finally met Bobby's, unblinking. "But you never taught me how to belong."

His voice hardened, not with anger, but with finality. "And that," he said as the city stirred to life around them, "is the future you're about to see."

Bobby stood frozen, surrounded not by ruins, but by the echo of a family he had dismantled slowly, carefully, and without ever realizing what he was destroying.

The ground crunched beneath Bobby's feet, and the world began to tilt, pulling him deeper into hell.

Suddenly, the ground steadied beneath Bobby's feet, though his stomach still churned in turmoil. He blinked again, and the wreckage of the blown-up intersection was replaced by a different reality. Now he was in what should have been a bustling airport.

The silence was terrifying. Planes remained stationary on the runway. A group of passengers filed out the door, eyes blank, luggage abandoned.

A frantic voice resounded through an intercom. "All flights are canceled indefinitely. Navigation systems are offline."

Expressionless, Bobby's son stood there. "Without GPS calculations, planes do not fly. Trucks do not make deliveries on time. All roads America depends on are difficult to navigate and confusing since everyone relies on outdated maps."

A businessman knelt on the ground as he yelled into his phone. A mother clasped her child to her, mumbling that they'd never see home. Bobby felt the weight of it—not theoretical, not afar, but near. The world could not run without direction.

"Impossible," Bobby breathed to himself, his voice hardly making it out. "Maps still exist. People can adapt."

Daniel glared at him with his dark eyes. "Don't you understand? The rhythm of your world, the connections that you are so proud of, were all founded upon GPS navigation. Surely without it, you are lost."

The scene shifted again, and they were in a hospital. There was a stale smell. Hallways were lined with patients groaning on stretchers. Physicians rushed past with sweat dripping from their foreheads and their hands trembling.

Bobby grasped his son's arm. "Why here? What is it about this place?"

His son held up his hand, indicating a blood bank door that was open. Shelves were bare. Plastic bags of plasma were ruined, yellow, and worthless. A doctor cursed and slammed the door shut.

"This vital invention found ways of storing and separating blood," said his son. "He built the first massive blood bank. Thousands of soldiers were saved because of him. But in this world, the blood spoils. The surgeries fail. The mothers die giving birth. The children bleed to death from accidents. This is what you chose when you said their work didn't matter."

Bobby's breath hitched. His own memories tugged at him—being rolled into the ambulance, Marcus's jacket pressed against his wound, his life held in the balance. He saw with horror that if not for that invention, he would have died already.

He shook his head wildly. "This is cruel. You're playing games with me."

But Daniel only said, "You are seeing what happens when you take away truth."

A cry caught Bobby's attention and pulled him to another ward. He ran in the direction of the sound and saw a doctor holding the small hand of a child. The boy's skin was white, his chest hardly moving. "We have nothing left," the doctor gasped. "The incubator broke."

His son's voice was one of a harsh verdict. "The portable incubator saved hundreds of premature infants. Without it, infant mortality rates would be much higher, and healthy development would be at greater risk."

Bobby cringed, grasping his chest. His empire, his speeches, his vanity—none of it could salvage the premature infant in the nursery.

The hospital walls dissolved into another horror. He was on a crowded street full of coughing as loud and rhythmic as machine-gun fire. People's faces were covered with scraps of cloth, but fear glowed in their eyes. A nurse rushed past him, her hands uncovered.

"The masks," Bobby gasped, understanding.

Daniel nodded. "Another lost invention that provided the world with the N95 mask. Its science protected millions during our pandemic. Without it, disease runs wild. Hospitals are destroyed. Countries crumble."

Bobby ached to yell. He had mocked Marcus for having a mask on once. Now he watched streets strewn with bodies, families carrying their dead wrapped in blankets. He held his hand against his face, as if he could cover the smell of illness.

"Enough," he croaked. "Enough!"

But his son mocked him.

And then they entered a dark office building. Desks were empty, computers cold. A technician hammered at a screen in vain, wires dangling, nothing moving. "It's gone," she told him. "Everything."

Daniel swept his hand across the vacant machines. "A Black engineer helped bring the personal computer into being. An Indian American scientist gave you the USB device, the connection that held your virtual universe together. Without them, your data empire collapses. No telecommuting, no e-commerce, no email, no servers. Phillips Media never got off the ground, and neither did your fortune."

Bobby spun, his heart pounding. His own office existed for an instant, deserted, monitors dark. Rosa's work disappeared, her brilliance erased. His empire was reduced to ashes.

"The world you scorned as meaningless now keeps silent."

Sobbing, a teenage girl hit a lifeless screen. "Where's the music? Where are the videos?" she cried.

The quiet was stifling. Even Bobby, who once mocked YouTube as foolish, yearned for it like a weight on his chest.

His son had an outburst, saying, "The iPod never existed. The music culture that supported generations is gone. Songs don't migrate. Voices are silenced."

The streets grew dark, the silence thick. Bobby wished he could cover his ears, get away from the emptiness. But every corner revealed another missing person, another crumbling of the world he once thought was safe.

Casting his shadow over the rubble, his son loomed over him. "Do you see, Father? All the amenities you so easily took for granted were issued from hands you discarded. You instructed them to depart. You told them their labor did not matter. This is what remains when they depart."

Bobby knelt, truth suffocating him. Behind him lay a starving world, a world that was sickened and silenced. And within the silence, his son's words resonated like a curse:

"This is the America you wished for."

Bobby's chest heaved as though he'd run miles. The silence that followed his son's words was worse than the noise before. Desperate to escape from the wreckage around him, he stumbled to his feet.

"Stop it," he pleaded, his voice hoarse. "I see. I understand. You've made your point."

Daniel did not answer. He raised a white hand, and the universe formed itself once more.

Bobby now stood before a skyscraper he recognized immediately. Its glass facade once proudly reflected the city's skyline. It was his jewel, Phillips Media headquarters. Its doors now hung open, its lobby dark and dusty. The banners of his empire hung in tatters.

Empty rows of desks filled the interior, the computer monitors dark. Papers littered the floor. A once thriving newsroom sat quiet, its lights cold. A calendar on the wall was outdated years ago.

"This is your legacy," his son recited.

Bobby moved his head with intensity. "No. My firm was thriving. We had the best talent, the best ideas."

His son's voice was as cold as steel. "Your best ideas were never yours. There were no computers, USB devices, or virtual content for your workers to create and collaborate. There was no innovation to save your empire without Rosa, whose work you stole. The innovations of the workers you laid off kept your company in business. Without them, Phillips Media never rose. Without them, it fell."

Bobby lurched through the empty newsroom. On one of the desks was a newspaper that was cracked and yellowed. He picked it up and squinted at the cover, which read, *Phillips: A Name of Greed and Failure.*

His gut dropped. Underneath was a photo of his face, not smiling but sneering, a parody of disdain. The article referred to him as the man who mocked diversity, who disparaged the workers who carried his empire, who lived blind to the world until it fell beneath him.

"This isn't true," Bobby said, even though his voice shook. "This can't be how they remember me."

Daniel stood towering behind him. "History recalls what you leave behind. And you left only scorn."

The building dissolved into the street outside, but the rest of the city that surrounded it was not vibrant. Billboards wore blank faces. Stores closed their doors. Piles of garbage towered, untrod. Bobby staggered through a traffic light that dangled innocently over an empty intersection. Rats slithered along cracked sidewalks.

And then he heard voices, not chanting this time but children's voices.

He took a turn and saw them clustered in an alley. They were thin, gaunt, their clothes in shreds. Their eyes lacked any spark of curiosity or rebellion, only despair. One boy clutched a shattered tablet, its screen splintered, its wiring dead. Another girl, her face streaked with tears, hugged a doll stuffed with pieces of cloth.

Bobby's throat tightened. "Why . . . why do they look like that?"

His son stepped forward, pointing at the children. "Because hope is lost. The inventions, the ingenuity, the boldness, the brilliance—lost. And without them, the children had nothing to inherit."

Bobby's heart shattered as he saw his own daughter in the crowd. She was older now, but she still had the same eyes, which were bright at one time but now dull from starvation. She looked straight through him, not acknowledging him.

"No," Bobby panted. "No, that can't happen. My children would be safe. My money would make them safe."

His son's voice thundered. "Your wealth was built on sand. Without the pillars that you turned away from, it fell. You cannot buy hope, Father. And without hope, your own children and grandchildren are lost too."

The world tilted again, and Bobby found himself in a cemetery. The grass was uncut, the headstones askew. Grave upon grave extended into the mist. He stumbled between them until he saw one stone at the far end, shattered and desolate. It bore his name: *Bobby Phillips.*

No flowers stood in front of it. No footprints disturbed the ground. No mourners had come to cry. Only weeds sprouted, twisting through the crevices.

Bobby flung himself onto the earth, clawing the ground. "No. This is not how it happens. I'm remembered. I matter. My name holds worth!"

Giant and unyielding, his son towered above him. "You are remembered as a warning. Your name is spoken in revulsion. You were the cautionary story of pride, the guy who ignored the truth until it killed him."

Bobby cried out, the sound ringing through the empty cemetery. "Please. Please, say there is a chance. Say this is not inevitable."

His son came forward for the first time. His eyes blazed with something less than compassion and more than judgment. His voice was deep, heavy. "You said nothing when the crowd yelled the racist chant, 'Go back to your country.' Sometimes silence encourages outrageous behavior. Be careful of what you wish for, Father. You didn't think you needed them. You wanted their silence. And now you pay the price. Now all of them are gone, and your world is in utter chaos."

Bobby clutched the ground, his hands dirty, his fingernails broken. "No. I take it back. I see now. I was blind, but I see. Please . . . give me another chance."

His son stood tall. "The chance is not mine to give. It is yours to seize, if you dare."

And with those words, the ground tore beneath Bobby. Darkness engulfed him completely, and the tombstone above melted into the mist.

He plunged into darkness, his cries echoing, "I will change! I will change!"

And then nothing.

Chapter 8

The Grave

The world blurred once more, and the earth beneath Bobby softened and chilled. The choking stench of rot from the ruined city vanished, replaced by damp air heavy with moss and decay. He opened his eyes to stare at the tilting headstones.

It was a cemetery, but not one he had ever witnessed. The graves stretched out as far as he could see, row upon row of cracked marble and leaning crosses. Weeds wrapped around the markers, choking ivy, strangling names etched so faintly they could barely be read. The silence here was suffocating—not the absence of sound, but the absence of life. No birds. No insects. No wind whispering through the grass.

Bobby shuddered and wrapped his arms around himself. His grown son's form loomed a few paces ahead of him, still silent, still unmoving, his presence colder than the fog that crawled low along the ground.

"Why here?" Bobby cried out, his voice breaking as it rebounded off the stillness. "Why bring me here?"

His son said nothing. He merely turned, extending one arm to the endless sea of graves.

Bobby's legs carried him forward despite the anger rising in his chest. He passed by one marker where the name had nearly been erased. Only a trace of letters remained: *Charles Drew*, and below it were the words *Blood Pioneer*. The place was overgrown with weeds, no flowers, no flags, nothing to show a nation remembered the man who had saved its soldiers and people.

Bobby stumbled. He had just seen the hospitals without Drew's techniques. And now, to see his grave unkempt, neglected—it emptied his stomach.

Bobby's eyes darted from stone to stone. Wherever he looked, the names of the people he had known only in visions were there. Their graves were devoid of offerings, their names oxidized into anonymity.

"This is wrong," Bobby muttered. "These people were significant. They gave so much. They . . . they don't deserve to be abandoned like this."

The silence was finally broken by his son's voice, low and dense as the fog itself. "They were forgotten because men like you believed they were disposable. You built monuments to yourselves and left no room for theirs."

Bobby spun, anger fighting through his fear. "I didn't bury them! I didn't erase their names!"

His son's eyes were persistent. "But you lived as if they never existed. That is how forgetting begins."

Bobby's breath was shallow, his chest heaving up and down. He stumbled backward, his heel catching on a stone. He landed hard on the damp earth, his hands brushing moss. He looked back at the headstone he had tripped over. The graves were bare, another set of names taken by the weeds.

He fought to his feet, his suit muddy. His son came forward, each step hesitant, calculated, the mist churning around him.

"This is more than a cemetery," his son said, his voice quiet and solemn. "It is America when memory is severed. It is the fate of all people who are denied their contributions. Their names perish, their deeds rot, and those who come after inherit nothing."

Bobby's mouth was dry. He wanted to argue, to protest, but his voice wouldn't come. He could only follow as his son pulled him deeper into the graveyard.

The graves crowded together here, packed so closely they strangled one another. The markers bore no names, only blank marble slabs. Bobby ran his hands over one, then another. "Who . . . who are these?"

His son's eyes were depthless shadows. "These are the nameless ones. The laborers, the workers, the farmers. Their blood and sweat constructed the cities, paved the highways, and fed the families. They were never carved into your history. Now they are here, forgotten even from memory."

Bobby was flailing. He bumped into one rock, his vision blurring. He tried to picture the skyscrapers he had seen in his dreams, the farms and roads, the schools and hospitals. All built upon backs he had ignored. And here, they were unmarked. Abandoned.

A gentle breeze began to blow. It whispered voices he could not place. He tilted his head and realized they were chanting. Not in anger, not in triumph, but in sorrow.

"We were here. We were here. We were here."

The words slithered through the fog, winding around him, pulling him deeper into sorrow. His son's hand lifted again, pointing across the graveyard.

Bobby's gaze followed his pointing finger. At the edge of the graveyard, half hidden in brambles, stood a bigger headstone. It was darker, more imposing, and cracked down the middle. He couldn't make out the name from where he was, but a surge of fear rose in his stomach.

His legs were heavy, but they moved him on nonetheless, step by unwilling step. The fog thickened and the whispers mounted, growing louder and louder, until his ears rang with them.

"We were here. We were here. We were here."

He halted a few steps away. His knees weakened. He knew which name his eyes would read before he saw it.

The chant was broken by the voice of his son, cutting through the air like a blade. "This is the grave you came to see."

Bobby shook his head, his lips trembling. "No. Please. Not that. Not mine."

Yet he could not stop. The stone loomed before him, its face etched with a name he could no longer evade.

Bobby Phillips.

Jagged and unforgiving, the stone towered over him now. The face of the stone was marred with lines of cracks, as if the ground itself had tried to tear it in two. Weeds sprouted at its base, climbing up the sides like hands reaching to crush the last shreds of memory from life.

Bobby gasped in jagged breaths. His eyes traced the letters carved deep into the stone:

Bobby Phillips
1969–20xx

That was it. No epitaph. No loving words, no respectful phrases. His name and two dates, the second not quite finished as if history was yet to be determined.

He collapsed to his knees, the wet earth seeping through his trousers. "No," he breathed. "No, this is not how it ends. This cannot be my resting place."

His son was behind him, quiet as the fog.

Bobby scratched at the weeds with frantic fingers, tearing them out of the foundation of the stone. The roots retaliated, slapping back against him and drawing welts. He stripped the moss from the letters, breaking his fingernails. But even when the name was legible, there was no consolation. The emptiness of it screamed more loudly than abandonment.

"This is incorrect," Bobby pleaded, his voice cracking. "I built an empire. I led men. I . . . I left something behind. Something more than this can't remain of me."

His son's shadow fell over him. "Empires based on pride crumble. Names etched in vanity are erased. You set aside those who stood behind you, and when they were swept away, so were you."

Bobby rested his forehead on the chilly stone, his own breath clouding on it. His mind whirled with visions—boardrooms filled with executives, his words from speeches quoted in the papers, photographs of himself on glossy magazine covers. He had seen his name etched into history with dignity. And here it rested, alone and hated.

In the fog, shadows shifted. Figures took shape, their outlines unclear, their faces hidden. They drew near, speaking words that cut more keenly than blades.

"Greed."

"Blindness."

"Arrogance."

"Theft."

Bobby spun around, terror surging in. "No! That is not true! I worked harder than anyone. I earned what I had!"

But the voices grew louder still, the whispers swelling into a chorus.

"You mocked us."

"You erased us."

"You stole what we gave and claimed it as your own."

The shadows approached, their forms jerking like smoke. Some of them carried instruments—hammers, shovels, pens, and tools. Bobby recognized them. A pilot's helmet, a soldier's rifle, a builder's glove, and a nurse's cap. They were the very people whose graves he had passed—the workers, the protectors, the inventors.

One shadow huddled low, its face inches from his. Its eyes glowed faintly, but its mouth was not there. "You lived as if we were invisible. Now you are the one unseen."

Bobby screamed, turning around until the back of his head hit his own gravestone. The stone chilled his spine, pinning him in place as the circle closed.

"Stop," he begged. "Please. I didn't know. I didn't mean—"

His son's voice cut through, thick and unmerciful. "You didn't want to know. Ignorance was your solace, pride your shield. And this is your legacy."

Bobby's knees buckled. He braced against the rock, sobs convulsing his chest. His empire had already been shown to him in ruins. His children, without hope. His name, cursed and reviled. But this, in this graveyard, was the truth that finally seeped into his bones: he'd lived for legacy, yet had none.

No one comes here," Daniel continued. "No flowers. No footprints. Not even your people. Your children, who once wore your name proudly, have cast it aside. They know only your apathy and cruelty. They tell their children not of your triumph, but of your defeat. Your monument is not a thing of mourning. It is a warning."

Bobby raised his head. His tear-stained face reflected the dim light of the mist. "A warning?"

His son nodded once. "To every man who thinks himself better than the men who bore him. To every voice that quiets the chorus. To every leader who supposes legacy can be forged without thanks."

The words struck with a hammer's force. Bobby clenched the stone, his fingers hurting from the thorns wedged into the weeds. He could protest, argue, cling to even one strand of pride. But there it was—proof in front of him. The graves of dead heroes. Nameless workers killed. His own children abandoning his memory. His own grave, broken and desolate.

The shadows withdrew into the fog as their whispers faded. But the voice of their condemnation echoed in his ears.

"Blind."

"Arrogant."

"Forgotten."

When the last voice fell silent, Bobby was alone again. Only his son remained with him, standing tall, his eyes fixed on Bobby with a mixture of shame and remorse.

Trembling, Bobby shoved his hands into the ground. "Tell me this is not the end," he panted. "Tell me there is more than this. Tell me that I can alter it."

His son was silent. He simply held up his hand, gesturing once again at the tombstone.

Bobby stood up to it again. His name caught fire against the rock, burning more fiercely than ever. He imagined folks walking by, smirking, and telling their kids, *"That is the man who squandered his chance. That is the man who ignored the truth until it killed him."*

His stomach knotted, the bile rising. He doubled over, vomiting onto the ground. The ground swallowed it instantly, leaving nothing, no sign that he had ever been there.

The desperation of it struck him harder than any blow.

He had once considered himself immortal by legacy. But legacies, he came to see now, were fragile things. They were not chiseled in glass spires or carved in newspaper headings. They were carved in memory, in appreciation, in the lives that were touched by modesty. And he had none of these.

The grave was still, but stillness screamed louder than famine visions or chaos or sickness. It spoke softly: *"You lived. You died. And the world didn't miss you."*

Bobby fell to the ground, and his body shook. He buried his face in the dirt at the bottom of the stone. His sobs echoed into the fog.

His body convulsing, Bobby crashed face-first in the dirt. His hands pushed against the ground at the foot of his gravestone as if the simple act of grasping it would somehow pull his name back into merit. The mist, curling like a shroud, grew more oppressive around him.

"Please," he spat harshly, his voice cracked and splintered. "Please, not this. Not here. I don't want this to be me."

Thick and unrelenting, the silence enveloped him. His son stayed behind him, a shadow, but spoke not one word of comfort. The silence judged.

Bobby forced himself to his knees. His suit was tattered, his face streaked with dirt and tears. He reached out, stroking the stone as if it would give. The cold granite bit into the tips of his fingers. "There has to be something left. Something I can do. Tell me it's not too late."

His son's voice, deep and flat, at last boomed in the fog. "You were warned. You looked to the past, the present, and the future. You looked to the world without their influence. You looked upon the children with no hope. And now, here, you look on your demise. This is the sum of your choices."

Bobby shook his head vigorously, his palms slapping into the ground. "No! I can do better. I will do better. I promise you. If you give me one more chance, I'll be better. I'll get it right. I'll treat them right. I'll treat all of them right."

His son tilted his head, the fire in his eyes glowing faintly. "You said such things before, in gentler terms. When workers asked to be heard, you promised to take them under review. When citizens cried for justice, you complained. Words are cheap. Legacy is action."

Bobby crawled out ahead, reaching for his son's knees like a beggar. "Then let me do it! Let me show you. I'll hire back the people I let go. I'll pay for their schools, their scholarships, their neighborhoods. I'll give Rosa her credit. I'll put their names on every building if necessary. Just let me do it. Let me make it right."

His son looked down at him sternly. The mist swirled, and the whispers were once more almost imperceptible. *"We were here. We were here."*

Bobby's cries were full of anguish. He thumped his fist on the ground. "Please! I don't want to die forgotten. I don't want my kids to curse me. I don't want this to be it."

The ground trembled. The headstone split further with a gruesome sound that resembled cracking bone. The split widened, and Bobby took a step back, staring in horror. Darkness seeped upward from the crack, spread across the weeds, and devoured the soil around it.

His son raised one hand to the monument. "Your legacy comes crashing down. The earth can no longer bear what was built on pride. This is the fate you engineered for yourself."

Bobby screamed and collapsed to the ground, his arms outstretched in desperation. "Then take it away from me. I don't care about legacy anymore. I don't care about my empire. I just want to live. I just want to make things right."

The crack widened. The coffin yawned like an open mouth, the earth tumbling into the void. Bobby clung to the edge, his fingernails tearing as soil slid out of his grasp. Screaming, he dangled over the void.

"I will change!" A cry tore from his throat, raw, animal-like. "I will change! I promise you, I won't waste another breath. I'll live differently. Please—please let me live!"

His son knelt on the edge of the cliff and stared down at him. There was a moment's silence, except for Bobby's ragged breathing and the creaking of the crumbling ground. And then, softly, Daniel said, "You have to mean it. Not for you. Not for legacy. But for them."

Yes!" cried Bobby. "For them! For the ones I despised, for the workers, for the families, for Marcus, for Rosa, for my children! I will not waste it again. I swear it."

The face of his son did not shift, but the voice grew almost sorrowful. "Then let this be your last chance."

The tomb snarled at him. The blackness bubbled like mist, swirling around his arms, his legs, pulling him down. He screamed, holding against the pull. "No! Not yet! Please! I'll change, I'll—"

The fog thickened, swallowing his words. The cemetery spun. The blackness tightened, muttering once more. *"We were here. We were here. We were here."*

Bobby's hand slipped. The emptiness pulled him down. For a moment, he was suspended, falling through endless dark, his screams echoing on forever. He thought it would save him. He thought he was lost.

Then—light.

A flash of light appeared, sharp and blinding. He gasped for air, his lungs agonizing as if he'd been drowning. Abruptly, the graveyard vanished, the fog cleared, and the shadows drew back.

The last thing he heard, just before everything faded, was his son's gentle and final words.

"Live differently . . . or die forgotten."

Chapter 9

Transformation and Redemption

Bobby's eyes opened to white haze. The ceiling above him hummed softly with fluorescent lights, their antiseptic glow fading at the periphery of his vision. His throat was raw and dry, his flesh burning as if afire. His chest sank and rose gradually, each breath labored as if weights rested on his breast.

For an instant, he was sure he was in the graveyard. The silence was the same. The heaviness still weighed over him. The smell of disinfectant mixed with the smell of damp earth.

Then the beeping started. The soft, insistent beat of a monitor by his bed reminded him that he was alive. *Alive.* The word was tinged with relief and terror.

He tried to talk but could only manage a rasp. His lips moved to form his son's name, but nothing came out. He cautiously turned to the side, expecting that he would find his loved ones nearby—his children, perhaps even co-workers who had gotten along with him. That was how he always imagined it, how he always expected it would be when his time came.

There was just one chair occupied.

Clara, his executive assistant, sat there scrolling absently through her phone. A plastic cup of coffee steamed beside her. Her eyes lifted at the sound of his movement, but they did not widen with relief. They didn't fill with tears or joy.

"You're awake," she said simply, her tone flat, professional.

Bobby gulped hard, his throat parched. "Where . . . where is everybody?" he croaked. His voice was rough, like it would be if he pulled it down a pipe.

Clara put her phone down and placed her hands in her lap. "Everybody?" she asked, raising an eyebrow.

"My family, peers, my staff." His voice broke. His eyes searched her face for comfort, wishing she would tell him they had only gone out and would be back soon. But the truth weighed in her silence.

Clara settled back in the chair, a stoic expression on her face. "No one came to see you, Mr. Phillips. Not your children. Not your cousin. Not your peers. Your nurses said a few peers and employees asked about you, but none of them wanted to come. Truthfully, most people thought . . . they hoped . . ." She didn't finish the sentence.

Bobby's stomach rolled. "Hoped?"

She gazed at him directly. "That you would never wake up."

The words cut deeper than any blade. He winced, his face turning from her, but the reality pressed on him from all sides. The stillness outside his hospital room, the lack of bouquets, and the silence all bore witness to what she'd said.

"I don't believe you," he breathed, but his own voice was a betrayal.

Clara's tone was not cruel, but it was not soft either. It was firm. "Hard to believe, but that's the truth. I did not come because the world could not survive without you. I came because I still need my job. I have a child to provide for, a special-needs son. Between his therapies, his treatment, and the bills, this paycheck is the only thing I'm using to put food on the table for him. That's the only reason I stayed."

Bobby blinked, stunned. He had worked with Clara for years. She was efficient, always on time, always prepared. He had thought of her as furniture to his empire, useful but unseen. Never once had he asked after her family. Never once had he cared.

"You . . . you have a son?" His voice collapsed, weak with disbelief.

Clara's lips blanched to a thin line. "Yes, I do. He's seven. Bright, kind, enjoys crosswords. But he needs more than I can possibly give him alone. So, I hold on to this job, no matter how loudly you scream or jeer. Because the paycheck pays for his future."

Bobby stared at her, the machines beeping steadily on either side of him. Her words were bricks. The graveyard images crowded back into his head—the faceless graves, the forgotten children. And Clara, a woman he had walked past each day without seeing, was fighting her own silent war.

"I didn't know," he whispered, his voice shaking.

"You never asked," she replied.

The silence lingered between them for a long time. Bobby's eyes flicked open, his chest struggling to breathe. He had begged in the cemetery for second chances, had vowed he would live differently. Now that he lay in this bed, he saw how empty his life had been. No one wanted him to live. No one except for the woman who hadn't had the choice but to sit there.

"I thought . . . I thought I meant something," he whispered.

Clara didn't relent. "You meant something to yourself. The rest of us? We only mattered when it benefited your image."

Bobby's tears dripped down his temples onto the thin pillow under his head. He hadn't cried in years, not since he was little. His sobs were soft, splintered, nothing like the boastful orations he used to make.

"I was wrong," he whispered. "Everything. I was blind."

Clara stood looking at him, her face inscrutable. For the first time, there was a glimmer of something—not sympathy, not pardon, but perhaps curiosity.

"You've had a lot of time to be wrong," she said. "What are you going to do now that you're awake?"

Bobby's mind flashed with visions: the crowded hospitals, the vacant schools, his crumbling empire, the tomb bearing his name. His son's words whispered back to him: *"Live differently, or die forgotten."*

"I don't know," he admitted, his voice frail. "But I won't squander this. Not again."

Clara was quiet afterward. She returned to her coffee, scrolling once more on her phone, providing him no solace, no warmth. But her words lingered in his mind like fire.

The door groaned ajar, and a few hospital personnel edged through, clipboards poised, still sporting the furrows of their masks. A Black nurse retightened his IV line with professional ease. A Latino resident flipped through the chart. An Asian doctor recited information from the monitors, his voice calm but accurate.

Bobby coughed, the sound dry, unfamiliar. "How, how long was I out?" he croaked.

The nurse glanced up. "A few days," she murmured. "You experienced a lot of trauma. We transfused you with several liters of blood. You're stable now, but it was touch-and-go."

Blood. That was the word that hit him. He remembered the name from Eleanor's visions—Dr. Charles Drew, the doctor whose blood banks had saved thousands during the war. And now, in the quiet of a modern hospital, Bobby realized Drew had saved him too.

Later that afternoon, Bobby asked to speak directly with the attending doctors. Two doctors entered, along with a nurse who was taking his vitals while they reviewed his chart.

"You sustained a severe concussion and a spinal injury," one of them explained. "The impact would have been fatal if you hadn't been treated so quickly at the scene. Your driver—Marcus, wasn't it?—kept your airway clear, stabilized your head, and controlled the bleeding. If it hadn't been for him, you'd be dead."

Bobby grasped the blanket, the truth striking him with more force than the pain in his back. "So the cane . . . ?"

"It's temporary," the second doctor reassured him. "You'll require it when you're recovering, but through therapy, you ought to regain strength."

Bobby nodded slowly. His eyes closed as he took in their words. For the first time, he understood how near he had come to leaving the world unloved, unremembered—and how the man he had mocked had saved his life.

Weariness pulled at him, heavier than the IV drip in his veins. His eyelids fell, hospital voices fading into the hum of machinery. As he slipped into unconsciousness, one truth remained clear: he would never again be the man who had entered that gala. His former life was gone.

For the first time in years, Bobby Phillips slept silently, not triumphantly or arrogantly, but bare.

The morning sun filtered through the blinds of the hospital, pale and weak, painting stripes on Bobby's bed. He had not slept. The hours crept by as he lay there, replaying Clara's statements and the ghostly apparitions that seemed to pursue him throughout eternity. Each time he let himself shut his eyes, he saw the shattered gravestone baring his name in his mind. Each time he breathed in Daniel's warning: *"Live differently, or die forgotten."*

When Clara came in with a fresh cup of coffee and a folder tucked under her arm, Bobby shifted position. His tone was gentle but firm. "Clara," he said.

She stared at him for a moment, setting the cup on the bedside table. "Yes?"

"Sit, please."

She arched an eyebrow but humored him after shoving the chair closer.

"I've been thinking," Bobby began, his words measured unlike the practiced speeches he once gave, "about what you said. About your son."

Clara's shoulders stiffened a little. "What about him?"

"I never asked," Bobby explained, shame infusing his voice. "Never cared. And yet you remained. You endured me for his benefit. I can't undo all the years that I didn't care, but I can do something now."

He shifted, wincing at the tug of the IV. "Effective immediately, you're getting a raise. You're getting a merit increase in your salary and a significant spot bonus for your commitment and hard work. Enough to cover whatever therapies, whatever schooling, whatever he needs. I'll have it drawn up today."

Clara's eyes widened in shock. Then a small, disbelieving chuckle escaped her mouth. "You're joking. You've spent years threatening to withhold people's paychecks if they make another typo, Bobby. You made Rosa redo her whole project just to be frugal. Now you're increasing my salary and giving me a bonus!"

Bobby looked at her and responded, "Yes. Because you and your son deserve it and because I can't stand by anymore, pretending like I built this empire in solitude. I didn't. People like you bore it, while I enjoyed the accolades."

Clara gazed at him for a moment, hunting his face for the sarcasm or viciousness that usually underlay his words. But there was none. Only a quivering sincerity that she had never seen.

"Fine," she replied finally, her tone softer but wary. "I'll believe it when I see it."

"You will," Bobby promised.

He leaned back, breath trembling, but a curious lightness filled his chest. For once, he'd not barked commands or demanded applause. He'd tried, in a small way, to give.

The momentum carried him. "Clara," he said again. "Put Rosa on the line. Call Rosa."

Clara tilted her head. "Rosa? The engineer?"

"Yes."

A questioning look flashed across her face, but she produced her phone. After a quick tap of the keys, she offered her phone to him. "She's on."

Bobby hesitated, holding the phone clumsily, the IV tugging at his arm. "Rosa," he began, his voice trembling.

There was a pause on the other end. "Mr. Phillips?" The voice was guarded, wary.

"Yes. It's me. Listen—I have to say something. No, I have to say lots of things."

Another silence. He imagined she was scowling with folded arms.

"I stole your idea," he admitted. The words stung, but they were said. "That invention you came up with, the algorithm that filtered out our streams of media. I used it for the company. I made millions, and you worked part-time evenings just to make ends meet. I was stupid. Worse, I was cruel."

The silence stretched on. Bobby shook as he held the phone.

"I can't undo the past," he said finally. "But I can do better from here forward. I already spoke with legal. We'll file a correction so your name gets added to the patent. You'll become a director with stock options and a salary adjustment. And you'll receive a significant spot bonus for the work you should have received as an award years ago. Above all, everyone will know that you developed the algorithm. The credit will finally be yours."

Rosa's bitter laugh was tainted with doubt. "Is this a joke? Did Clara put you up to this?"

"No," Bobby whispered. "It's me. I'm saying it because it's true. And I'm begging you—don't think I'm doing this for me. I'm doing it because I know what happens when people don't do the right thing."

The line stayed quiet for a very long time. Then Rosa spoke, her voice softer. "I don't know what's gotten into you, Mr. Phillips. But if this is real, if you're serious . . . then thank you. It's long past due."

"It is," Bobby said, his throat tightening. "More than you know."

His hand trembling, he thrust the phone at Clara. She slipped it into her pocket as she regarded him with new eyes.

"You sound like a man who has just seen a ghost," she growled.

Bobby shut his eyes, remembering the headstone, the shadows, his son's voice. "I saw more than ghosts," he whispered.

The remainder of the day was a blur of phone calls. Clara, always dubious, began making phone calls for legal papers for Rosa's promotion, bonus, and acknowledgement. Bobby told her to schedule a meeting with the board and add several things to their next agenda.

"We need a scholarship for our employees."

He gave orders, yes, but there was no arrogance, no condescension. Only a sense of urgency, as though he was racing against time.

When Clara came to a stop, staring at him in amazement, he smiled feebly. "You asked what I would do since waking up. This is it. I will use what is left of life to uplift others, not me."

Clara did not roll her eyes or bristle for offense this time. She just nodded, quietly, as if considering the possibility that he might actually mean it.

Later, when the hospital room darkened into night, Bobby lay back against his pillow. Weary, his body was still weak, but his heartbeat in a different way—not with ambition's thudding, but with the trembling of a man who'd been reprieved.

The recollection of his son's final warning echoed through his mind: *"Live differently, or die forgotten."*

For the first time, Bobby believed that he could.

By the end of the week, it had spread. The gossip ran through the Phillips Media corridors like a spark. Rosa had been given a promotion and a company award announcement—a headline no one ever imagined they'd read. Clara's raise was a rumor, then whispered reality. Rumors that the board would be discussing the launch of a scholarship fund spread quickly around the office, stirring surprise in departments where staff had long grown used to austerity and reductions.

Employees traded whispered rumors at elevator banks, in breakrooms, and during rapid lunches.

"What is he doing?" one man asked, his voice filled with suspicion.

Another shrugged. "Maybe he's trying to buy back his soul. Don't believe it."

A third, younger employee, whispered, "Suppose he really means it?"

The skepticism was well-founded. Bobby Phillips had nurtured fear masking as loyalty for decades. But as days passed, rumors became louder, until at last he arranged a company-wide videoconference from his hospital room. The camera framed him, propped up against white pillows, his color pale, a cane leaning against the bedside. Before the meeting began, he had spoken with his doctors about when he might safely leave the hospital. The concussion and back injury would keep him there for a while, they warned. For now, this was the only way to reach his employees.

The press release surprised them most of all. Bobby barely talked to the whole staff, other than to announce record profits or sweeping layoffs. Some complained it was just another PR stunt, a publicity gesture to whitewash his image after the crash. Others came because they wanted to see what new firestorm would erupt.

The auditorium gradually filled. Employees' seats were held fast, their conversation strained. In Bobby's hospital suite, Clara sat nearby with her clipboard, taking notes as the videoconference link connected. Her gaze shifted between Bobby on the bed and the monitor that displayed the growing crowd of employees. She had seen the papers filed, heard the sincerity of his voice, but even she wasn't sure what would happen when he spoke to hundreds at one time.

On the big screen in the auditorium, Bobby appeared. He sat propped against a stack of pillows. His hospital gown was hidden beneath a blazer Clara had insisted he wear, but he still looked gaunt, his cheeks hollow, his hair thinner than most remembered. For the first time, his employees saw not the untouchable executive but a man humbled, fragile.

The room went silent. His height and swagger were gone. His voice when he began, however, carried with strength.

"I know what you're waiting for," he began. "Another sermon on profits. Another lecture on working harder, sacrificing more, receiving more. That's what I've presented to you previously. Cold words. Demands. No thank you."

The workers shifted uneasily. His honesty unnerved them more than his usual haughtiness.

Bobby took a deep breath, winning faintly. "I must tell you something I've never told you." He paused and then said, "I was wrong."

The silence became denser. A buzz traveled around the back row but was quickly swallowed by the weight of the situation.

"I built my career on the premise that I was the master builder of this company's success," Bobby stated. "That my vision alone kept us afloat. I undervalued you as disposable, as static to my brilliance.

I even attributed inventions, ideas, and work to myself that weren't mine. I diminished diversity. I mocked movements for justice. I acted like this empire was founded on my name only. That was a falsehood."

Gasps echoed across the room. People gazed at each other, questioning if this was madness or confession.

Bobby's tone hardened as he went on. "This business is here because of you. Because of the heads and hands of people that I forgot. Rosa, whose work took us to the next level of innovation, not mine. Clara, who kept this company running when I mistreated her. Each engineer, each janitor, each assistant, each artist who put their heart and time into it. And I, in my ignorance, made that real. I cannot make up for the years I stole from you. But I can start now."

He hesitated, his gaze sweeping the lines of faces. Most looked back skeptically, but others stared in silent wonder.

From today forward," Bobby stated firmly, "Rosa will receive the credit and stock options she has earned. Scholarships are being set up for underrepresented youth. Salaries are being reexamined, starting with those who have worked the hardest and benefited least. And our annual celebration will honor every employee's contribution, not leadership's. Because this company was never mine. It was ours. It was yours."

A murmur swelled again, not of disbelief this time but of something more fragile. *Hope.*

One woman in the front row pressed a tissue to her eyes. A man in the middle row shook his head slowly, whispering, "I never thought I'd hear him say that." Others still sat rigidly, waiting for the catch, the insult, the sting.

Clara watched from the hospital suite, her heart squeezed. She had seen him annihilate men and women in meetings, watched his brutality take their dignity away. She now heard words she had previously fantasized he would say but never imagined would become reality. Her skepticism still existed, but for the first time, she allowed a crack of faith to grow.

On screen, Bobby's hand tightened around the edge of the blanket. His body trembled with weakness, yet his voice was firm. "I don't ask your forgiveness. I don't deserve it yet. All I ask is to be given the chance to demonstrate, by my actions, that I will live differently. That I will not waste what time I have remaining."

The stillness that followed was not chilly, not unfriendly. It was heavy, uncertain, but alive.

Slowly, hesitantly, a few of the staff began applauding. The applause was startlingly harsh in the auditorium. Hands continued to join the applause. The applause grew more confident, then certain, until the auditorium rang with a noise Bobby had never heard in response to him before—not forced, not fearful, but genuine.

Bobby lowered his head, shocked. He did not smirk smugly as he once had, did not bask in applause. He just nodded, his eyes welling with tears.

When the meeting ended, workers flowed out in subdued clusters, chattering about what they'd seen. Some shook their heads, certain it was a performance. Others held out the possibility that things might be different now.

Clara approached Bobby slowly. "I don't know what's happened to you," she said quietly. "But if you're telling the truth, then maybe—maybe—it isn't too late."

Bobby looked at her, his voice low but resolute. "It won't be just words anymore. You'll see."

That night, alone in his hospital bed, he stared at the ceiling. The applause was still ringing in his head, interwoven with the incantation from the cemetery: *"We were here. We were here. We were here."*

He spoke into the quiet, a promise to himself and to those unheard voices that had seen him through so far.

"This time, I will not waste it."

Chapter 10

A Nation United

Bobby did not wake with resolve.

Sleep came in fragments, shallow and restless, broken by images that refused to fade. Daniel's voice lingered in the spaces between breaths. Not shouting. Not accusing. Simply stating what had already been true long before the visions began.

"Be the best. No excuses. Second place means nothing."

He stared at the ceiling of the hospital room as dawn crept in through the blinds, the light thin and colorless. Machines, steady and indifferent, hummed beside him. Somewhere beneath the ache of his injuries, another weight pressed down, heavier than pain.

Recognition.

He thought of the empty city. The children with hollow eyes. The grave bearing his name, untended and forgotten. He had always imagined failure as collapse. Bankruptcy. Public disgrace. He had never imagined absence.

When he closed his eyes, he could still hear the chains. They did not tighten. They waited.

Bobby understood now that wanting to change was not the same as knowing how. There would be no grand absolution waiting at the end of good intentions. Whatever came next would be slower. Awkward. Uncomfortable.

And permanent.

By the time footsteps approached outside his door, Bobby had not found peace. But he had found responsibility.

The hospital stay continued for a few more days, long enough for Bobby to gain the strength to stand on his own once again. By the time the doctors were finally willing to release him, Clara was waiting with a folder full of appointments. But rather than the board meetings and investor calls that had filled his former life, the pages were filled with the names of schools, community centers, and museums.

"You instructed me to arrange it," Clara said as she walked beside him.

Bobby sat in a wheelchair, pushed by a hospital orderly toward the sliding glass doors. His cane rested across his lap, his posture stiff with lingering pain.

She continued. "These are places you said you wanted to support."

Outside, the car waited at the curb. The orderly braked gently, and Clara opened the door. Bobby shifted the cane into his hand, wincing as he rose with the orderly's help. Marcus steadied him from the other side, and together they eased him into the back seat. For the first time, Bobby met Marcus's gaze and said, "Thank you." Marcus's eyebrows furrowed, but he nodded.

As the vehicle pulled away from the curb, Bobby leaned forward slightly. "Marcus, how did you learn to do all that at the wreck? The first aid, keeping me alive until the ambulance came?"

Marcus kept his eyes on the road. "The military, sir. I was an Army medic prior to becoming a driver. Training does persist."

Bobby looked at him, his voice softer than usual. "So, what are you going to do with it then? I mean, if you weren't taking me around?"

Marcus hesitated for the first time, carefully choosing his words. "I want to attend paramedic school. Get certified. It's always been the idea, but . . . fees are expensive. With family to take care of, I just can't afford it now."

There was silence. Then Bobby's voice was soft. "You saved my life. Let me repay you. I'll pay it. Tuition, fees, whatever it is. You're too special to be driving this car when you can be saving lives."

Marcus's grip on the steering wheel tightened ever so slightly. His voice was controlled, practically incredulous. "You mean that?"

"I've never been more sure," Bobby said. "Consider it done."

Marcus breathed slowly, his head wobbling with incredulity. "Well, thank you, sir."

Bobby leaned back against the seat, wincing at the movement. "No, Marcus. Thank *you*. From now on, feel free to call me Bobby."

The ride was quiet. Bobby looked out the window, the skyline glinting in the afternoon sun. He realized he had only ever been impressed by his own victories, never by anyone else's. Now he wondered about the invisible hands that built them, about the names etched in history and the many more erased.

In his house, employees lined the doorway as Marcus escorted him in. Their smiles were polite, but their eyes held surprise. Bobby thanked them softly, gestures they found unnatural. Once he had passed, they nodded at each other. Something in the man had shifted.

Bobby retired early with his cane propped against the nightstand. On the bed, he sat and flipped on the TV. The light lit the room as the news reporter went on.

"Headlines in the news tonight."

Shelves in supermarkets, almost empty, were on the screen. Wilted lettuce, bruised apples, and expired milk cartons awaited no one. The caption read: *Consumers Have Fewer Choices as Farm Labor and Refrigerated Transportation Decline.*

The setting shifted to a crowded emergency room. Patients leaned against chairs, blankets draped over their shoulders, a mother cradling her screaming child. Caption: *Patients Wait Over 24 Hours as Physician Shortages Mount.*

Bobby's grip around the remote control tightened.

The final clip was a row of dark restaurants. Mexican, Chinese, Indian, seafood, all shut down. Handwritten signs read, *Closed.* Caption: *Worker Shortages Force Closures Nationwide.*

"Experts claim such shortages are growing critical. In the absence of solutions, industries threaten to collapse."

Bobby muted the sound, but the images lingered. Empty shelves. Families waiting endlessly. Restaurants gone dark. Bobby's mind raced. This was not a dream. Was this really happening now? His chest tightened as he recalled the children proudly naming inventors and farmers. Those contributions were unraveling before him.

"If this is what happens without them," he whispered, "then we're finished."

Exhaustion pulled him into a restless sleep.

By morning, light seeped through the blinds. Ache spread through his body, but his mind was made up. He would return to the office, not as master of the empire but as a man who was determined to fix it.

Bobby's return to Phillips Media was low-key. No cameras, no photo ops, no grand re-entry meant to impress. He walked through the glass doors with his cane and was greeted by neither applause nor tentative glances. Employees edged out of the way in the lobby, their murmurs directed to each other.

Before, Bobby would have relished their discomfort. Now, he was acutely aware of its weight. These were the people who had supported his business all these years while he basked in the spotlight. He owed them far more than apologies. He owed them action.

His first meeting on his return was not with shareholders or members of the board but with the employees themselves. He brought them to the cafeteria, the room filled with the hum of suspicion. Clara stood at his side, holding a clipboard in her hand, as Bobby worked his cane and began.

"I told you earlier that I was wrong," he said to them. "But words are hollow if they're not lived. Today, I come to demonstrate what I mean."

The workers looked at one another, expecting the punchline.

"First," he said, "all the workers who've lost their jobs in the past year will be offered their old positions back, along with a full salary review to ensure they are compensated fairly for their value. No more laying people off to make corporate bonuses. From now on, our performance-bonus structure will be reviewed and reformed to ensure it is fair, transparent, and rewards the contributions of all employees."

A murmur ran through the crowd. Some gasped, others frowned, not believing.

"Second," he went on, "we are working with the board to establish a scholarship fund for the children of our workers. Not only for managers or executives, but for all—from interns to janitors. Education is not a privilege reserved for a select few. It must be available for every family connected with this company."

This time, the murmur was accompanied by a sense of awe but also skepticism. One woman in the back covered her mouth with her hand.

"Third, we're working with minority-owned businesses," Bobby said. "Too often, contracts go to the same firms, the same cliques of privilege. That ends today. Our success will be built by opening doors, not closing them."

He paused and let the words sink in. "And finally, we will celebrate all of you. Not once a year with empty words, but every day, in how we treat one another. We are implementing an annual company celebration, but this year, it will be celebrating the people who push this company. Not me. Not the privileged. All of you."

The cafeteria grew silent for a considerable length of time. Then a maintenance worker raised his hand. "Why now? Why not years before?"

Bobby swallowed hard. "Because I was blind," he said with quietness. "Because I thought greatness took towers and headlines. I was wrong. Greatness is here, in this room, in you. I can't take back what I've done, but I can live differently now. That is all I can promise."

Hesitantly, slow clapping began at the edges of the room, but it moved. There wasn't clapping from everyone, but the sound became regular, a begrudging acknowledgment that something had shifted.

After the meeting, Bobby did not return to his office in the manner he once did. He walked down the halls, stopping to say hello to employees by name. He asked them about their families, their work, and their lives. He listened. When Rosa approached him, she stood tall, a mix of defiance and disbelief written plainly across her face.

"I read the documents," she said to him. "The patents, the credit, and the stock. You really did do it."

"I owed you that," Bobby replied. "And more."

Rosa looked at him. "I don't know if I can ever forgive what you did."

"You don't need to," Bobby told her gently. "Just know I will use what time I have left to see that no one else is treated like you were."

She nodded, still suspicious, but departed with the slightest hint of respect in her eyes.

Bobby sat in his study, cane propped against the desk, his body still aching from the accident. Papers were stacked in front of him— not board reports this time, but Clara's hospital files. The list she'd written glared back: school, community center, museum.

He grabbed the phone. "Clara, call them. Not for a photo op. I want to know what they actually need. No speeches. No photographers. Just ask, and I'll do it."

There was a pause. Then came Clara's voice, bordered by surprise. "You're serious?"

He was. "More serious than I've ever been."

She returned with answers the next week. The East Side School needed laptops and internet connections for the kids. "Done," Bobby said. "Every kid gets whatever they need."

The community center needed more tutors and staff to handle the children they sent away daily. "Hire them. Double their capacity."

The museum needed money to rescue exhibits of overlooked leaders and inventors. Bobby deliberated over the letter: *We just want their names remembered.* His throat tightened. "Write the check. No plaque with my name. This isn't about me."

Laptops were delivered within weeks, tutors were recruited, and renovations were in progress. No cameras, no ribbon cuttings. For the first time, Bobby gave without expecting applause.

Bobby's reforms didn't stop with the firm. In the next few weeks, he funneled money into neighborhoods. He funded after-school programs at the very community center he had attended. He donated anonymously to museums and charities for immigrants, vets, and disadvantaged kids. For the first time in his life, he gave without summoning cameras or waving checks in front of reporters.

Marcus, his chauffeur, noticed the difference especially one evening as he picked up Bobby from a meeting with a minority-owned firm. The car pulled away from the curb, easing into traffic as the city settled into its late-afternoon rhythm. Sunlight slanted between buildings, catching on windshields and crosswalk signs. Bobby stared out the window, quieter than usual since they had left the meeting.

The conversation replayed in his mind—the guarded optimism of the business owners, the way they chose their words carefully, the skepticism that sat behind every polite nod. They had heard promises before. He could feel it in the pauses.

Marcus drove in silence for several blocks, hands steady on the wheel, eyes forward. He had learned when to wait.

"Can I ask you something, Bobby?" he said finally.

Bobby shifted in his seat. "You can."

Marcus didn't look at him. "Was that meeting for show," he asked, "or did you really mean what you said back there?"

The question wasn't sharp. It wasn't accusatory. It sounded tired. Like a man who had seen sincerity borrowed too often and returned too late.

Bobby didn't answer right away. They slowed at an intersection. Pedestrians waited at the crosswalk—a mother tugging her child back from the curb, a delivery driver double-parked with his hazards flashing, a man on a bicycle balancing a stack of boxes. Ordinary people, moving the city forward.

"I'm still figuring that out," Bobby said at last. "But I'm trying to do it right."

Marcus nodded once. "Then meetings alone won't get you there."

Bobby turned slightly toward him. "What will?"

"Learning," Marcus said. "Real learning. Not the kind you get from reports or keynote speeches."

The car rolled to a red light. Bobby folded his hands, the silence no longer defensive. "Go on."

"There are places that tell the story you never heard," Marcus continued. "Not the fancy art museums you used to visit for society pages. I mean places that show how this country was actually built."

Bobby frowned slightly. "Such as?"

Marcus hesitated, then spoke with quiet certainty. "Places like the National Museum of African American History and Culture in Washington. The National Museum of the American Indian. The National Hispanic Cultural Center in New Mexico. The Japanese American National Museum. The Chinese American Museum out in Los Angeles."

The light turned green. The car moved forward.

Bobby leaned back, absorbing the names. "I didn't know half of those existed."

Marcus let out a short breath. "That's the problem. Most people don't."

Silence filled the car again, but this one felt different. Not hostile. Reflective.

After a moment, Bobby spoke. "What if kids could go there?"

Marcus glanced at him in the rearview mirror.

"I mean really go," Bobby continued. "Not just read about it online. Travel. Walk through it. See themselves in history instead of wondering where they fit."

Marcus said nothing.

"I sit on boards," Bobby went on. "And I work with minority-owned businesses now. What if we co-sponsored something? A scholarship. Expenses covered for high school students. They could write an essay about why learning this history matters to them."

The car drifted slightly before Marcus corrected course.

Bobby paused. "I could have Clara coordinate it. See what we can put together." He caught Marcus's eyes in the rearview mirror. "What do you think about that?"

Marcus blinked, genuine surprise crossing his face. "You really want my opinion?"

"Yes," Bobby said simply.

Marcus exhaled slowly, the tension in his shoulders easing. "I think it's a damn good idea. Kids need to see themselves in history. Need to know they come from something and can achieve something."

Bobby nodded. "Have you ever been to any of them?"

Marcus shook his head. "No. Couldn't afford it." He paused. "But during the pandemic, when schools shut down, I helped my kids with their schoolwork. We looked up those places online. Watched videos. Read articles. Learned more than I ever did in school." He smiled faintly. "YouTube turned into a classroom."

Then his voice grew thoughtful. "I tell my kids all the time—never stop learning. You're never too old to learn something new."

Bobby looked down at his hands, turning the words over slowly. "That's good advice," he said quietly. "Believe me, even at my age, I'm starting to take heed."

Bobby nodded. "Then we'll do it." He paused and said with a slight grin, "By the way, they will need chaperones, so you may get to visit some of them after all."

Marcus smiled and hesitated, then went on. "I enrolled in the paramedic course as you instructed. They accepted me into the spring class. Never thought I'd get the chance, but . . . now I have it."

Bobby turned to him, a small smile making its way at the corner of his mouth. "That's where you're supposed to be, Marcus. Saving lives isn't something that you simply do by nature—it's what you're supposed to do."

For the first time in a long, long time, Marcus's eyes softened. "Thanks to you, Bobby. I won't squander it."

The change in the company was apparent within a short period of time. Reemployed workers came back with relief stamped on their faces. Families forwarded scholarship requests for their kids, some with tears in their eyes. Minority-owned partners infused new vigor and concepts into the business.

And yet, Bobby remained in the background. He attended meetings but did not overshadow them. He signed checks but gave credit to those who deserved it. He stood when there was a time of celebration and clapped for others the loudest.

The company party didn't take place until several months later. Employees entered expecting another formal dinner, but instead found tables with photographs and stories of their own successes. Twenty years of service from a janitor. An engineer's innovation. A receptionist who had spent years mentoring new employees, guiding them through their first weeks.

Bobby was on the podium, not quite in the center of the light but slightly to the right. "Tonight is not about me," he stated flatly. "It never should have been. Tonight is about you. This company is nothing without you. And America is nothing without the people whose names have been forgotten through history but whose work built where we stand."

For the first time in history, the clapping was not obligatory, not courteous. It was authentic.

At the stage's edge, Clara was waiting for Bobby. "I never thought I'd live to see the day," she said, shaking her head.

"Neither did I," Bobby admitted. "But I think this is just the beginning."

He looked out at the crowd—a throng of different faces, clapping, smiling, hopeful. For the first time in his life, Bobby Phillips didn't think he was a king on a throne, but a man among men. And that, he knew, was worth more than any kingdom he had ever vowed to build.

The changes at Phillips Media persisted, and for the first time in decades, Bobby's empire was no longer shrinking but growing with focus. The building that previously shook with fear now contained an understated optimism. Workers who had kept their noses down for years began to look up. Corridors that were once filled with silence now buzzed with the sound of laughter, chatter, and the sense that people actually mattered.

And even while the company's public image was transforming, another truth weighed on Bobby. His family remained aloof, cut off by years of pride and neglect. His cousin Richard hadn't spoken to him since his accident. His college friend from way back, David, hadn't called him back in years. And most unfortunately, his own children had built a life where he was no longer included.

Now, sitting in his study on a cold evening, Bobby stared at his phone for what felt like an eternity before he dialed. His fingers trembled, not due to weakness but fear. Fear of silence, of rejection, of hearing it in their voices what he already knew—that he had failed them.

Richard answered on the third ring, his voice guarded. "Bobby?"

"It's me," Bobby croaked. "I need to see you."

There was a pause. Then, finally, "What for?"

Bobby replied, "I need to tell you something, face to face. Please."

Richard responded, "You're lucky I'm willing to listen to you."

They met in a dingy diner, the kind of establishment Richard liked to haunt and Bobby mocked. Bobby would mock its faded vinyl booths and plastic laminated menus, even going so far as to call it "a shrine to mediocrity." And now he sat in silence, cane leaning against the wall, the smell of fried onions and coffee keeping him grounded in humility.

Richard was already there, sipping coffee, his arms folded over his chest. He looked older than Bobby remembered, lines carved deep by years of disappointment.

"You're different," Richard said as Bobby slid into the booth.

"I am different," admitted Bobby. He breathed deeply, the words reluctant but true. "Richard, I made you feel worthless. I constantly reminded you that you were here only because of the family name. I belittled you when you attempted to warn me that I was going astray. I . . . I was cruel."

Richard regarded him for a moment, his own features a mask. "Why now?"

"Because I saw where it would lead." Bobby sighed. "I saw my grave. Empty. Unloved. Forgotten. I don't want that. I don't want my legacy to be cruelty. I want it to be change."

Richard's eyes softened, just a little. "You have a long way to go. But . . . maybe it's not too late."

The words were short, but to Bobby, they felt like the creak of an opening door that he thought was forever closed.

Bobby phoned David later. His calls, initially, went unreturned. He left messages—not the abrupt, assertive ones of earlier, but soft pleas. "It's not business. It's about us. Please."

Finally, after weeks, David agreed to meet with him.

"You've burned a lot of bridges, Bobby," David answered bluntly as they sat across from one another at a deserted coffee shop. His arms were folded, his eyes intense.

"I know," Bobby said. "But I'm not here seeking charity. I'm here to apologize. I took your partnership, your friendship, and I used it like something that could be discarded. You deserved better."

David leaned back, regarding him as if to assess whether this was a performance. "And now you want what from me?"

"Nothing," Bobby replied. "A chance to prove that I'm not the same man you walked away from."

David released a measured breath, his gaze narrowing. "We'll see."

It wasn't forgiveness, but it wasn't dismissal either. Bobby clung to that thread of hope.

The toughest reconciliations, though, were with his children. He had kept boasting that he was going to bring them money, but he had brought them neither warmth nor presence. Birthdays were forfeited to board meetings. Recitals were skirted for galas. He let their childhoods pass by, drowned out by the noise of his ambition.

His daughter visited him first, her arms crossed tightly as she entered his office, her heels clicking forcefully on the floor. "You think money can buy back the years you were away?" she charged. Her eyes flared, not with anger but with hurt.

"No," Bobby answered gently. "Money never could. I can't buy back the lost time. I can only plead to be in your life now, somehow, anyway you'll let me."

She stood frozen for a long time, then finally said, "We'll see."

Her response was identical to David's words, and it dawned on Bobby that all he deserved was a small crack in a wall he had built himself.

Then, when finally he sat across from his daughter and son, both of them, the weight pressed down more heavily. His daughter had already confronted him with birthdays and lost recitals. His son, quieter, had sat in the corner with folded arms.

Bobby turned to him, his voice trembling. "I had a dream," he said slowly. "In it, I saw what my life would look like if I didn't change. Empty halls. A grave no one visited. A legacy built on greed and nothing else. I had to make a choice to live differently or die forgotten."

Daniel's eyes widened and looked shocked, surprise breaking through his usual guarded expression. "You . . . dreamed that? I've wanted to say that to you for years."

"I did," Bobby admitted. "And it felt real. Too real. I don't want that ending. I don't want to be remembered that way. I want another chance. If you'll let me."

His son hesitated, studying him for signs of the man he had once despised. But what he saw now was different—not arrogance, but a plea. His father's words may be real, but time would tell.

Weeks passed. Slowly, Bobby began to express in deeds what words could not. He attended school events for his grandchildren, sitting in the back, clapping for recognition without seeking it. He visited Richard's home, no longer to boast but to listen. He met David for coffee, not as a business appointment, but he spoke of their childhood years instead. He asked about his children's lives and resisted the urge to advise.

He arrived. And arriving, he discovered, was something he had never actually done before.

Life was different by December. He was no longer the center of their universes, nor did he aspire to be. But he was welcomed back, not as dictator or figurehead, but as family.

During that holiday season, the city hosted a multicultural holiday festival in the downtown area. Bobby went with his grandchildren, not as a sponsor or guest of honor, but just as one face among the multitude of faces. He invited Clara and her son. They joined him along the festively decorated streets.

The wind was filled with laughter and music. Strings of lights glowed over the streets, bathing faces of every color in golden light. Vendors peddled food from everywhere on earth—steaming tamales alongside samosas, pies beside hummus and flatbread, and holiday sweets. Aromas merged into something rich and homey, a feast of cultures mixing together.

Children darted through and out of the throngs, their giggling rising over the hum of conversation. Bobby stopped to watch them, amazed at their freedom, their joy. For years, children had been in his eyes only as heirs, successors, extended segments of himself. Today, he saw them as they were—futures weighted with many inheritances, not just his.

On the main stage, a choir assembled, children of every background shoulder to shoulder. Bobby and Clara sat in the rear and their children sat toward the front of the stage. Waiting, Bobby rested his cane against his leg and folded his hands.

As the children began to sing, their voices mingled in harmony. No single voice stood out; each joined the others to become something greater than the individual parts. The music was joyful , strong, and vibrant.

Bobby's chest tightened as his mind flashed back to the shocking newscast when he arrived home from the hospital. He remembered the America he'd once envisioned—a shattered, barren America of no giving, no diversity, no oneness. And here before him, among the strangers who had become no longer strangers, he saw the contrary:

a vibrant, pulsating image of America's real greatness. Not one man, not one family, not one people, but all of them.

There was a stinging in his eyes. It was the first time in four decades that the tears did not spring from sorrow but gratitude.

Clara gazed at him, surprised to find him openly crying. "What's wrong?" she whispered.

Bobby wiped his face with the back of his hand. "I understand now," he said. "America ain't great because of guys like me. It's great because of them. Because of us, collectively."

The sound of the choir swelled on the stage, filling the coldness in the night air. Bobby sat in silence, no lights blinding, no words to say, no power to bargain. He was only one man among many, and he was thankful, unassuming, and serene.

He leaned forward slightly, making a final promise that only the winter wind could hear.

"I wasted so much. But I will not waste what's left. I will live differently and not die forgotten."

And for the first time in his own long, arrogant life, Bobby Phillips felt something he never had before. He felt complete.

About the Authors

Mack E. Smith and Sara Freeman Smith are independent publishers and authors dedicated to amplifying voices that demand to be heard.

Mack, an Honor Graduate of Southern University (B.S.) and University of Detroit Mercy (MBA), broke down economic barriers as a Relationship Manager with Chase Bank, helping African American professionals secure financing when other banks turned them away. His community service earned him the Silver Beaver Award from the Boy Scouts of America. He authored *How to Become a Mortgage Broker* when eBooks were just emerging.

Sara, an Honor Graduate of USC (B.A.) and University of Phoenix (M.A.), navigated corporate leadership while experiencing 90% vision loss. She served as Commissioner on the Houston Commission on Disabilities and received the J.P. Morgan Chase Leadership Fellows Award. She authored *Turning Stones into Gems: Finding Purpose in Your Life & Career.*

Together, they co-founded U R Gems LLC and co-authored *How to Self-Publish and Market Your Own Book,* empowering independent writers to share their stories.

A Nation Without: The History America Forgot channels their decades of advocacy into historical fiction confronting America's selective memory, exploring accountability and honoring the unsung heroes who built our nation.

Married 45 years with one son, daughter-in-law, and three grandsons, the Smiths live in Houston. Learn more about Mack and Sara Freeman Smith and their work at www.urgems.com.

Thank you for reading our book. We're so grateful for your time. We hope you found value in these pages, and our greatest compliment is you sharing this book with others. We would love to hear your feedback. Please contact us at info@urgems.com or scan the QR code below.

A Nation Without is just the beginning. We are constantly uncovering more stories of the diverse, unacknowledged men and women who shaped American history. To receive periodic exclusive newsletters into some of those contributors that history forgot, send us an email to info@urgems.com with the subject line "Forgotten" along with your name or scan the QR code below.